The Rewilding
Copyright © 2025
All rights reserved

Independently published

The characters and events portrayed in this book are fictitious. Any similarity to real persons, living or dead, is coincidental and not intended by the author.

No part of this book may be reproduced, or stored in a retrieval system, or transmitted in any form or by any means, electronic, mechanical, photocopying, recording, or otherwise, without express written permission of the publisher.

No part of this book, its cover or other related materials may be used for the training of Large Language Models (AI).

Print ISBN:9781037036767
Digital ISBN:9781037036774

Cover design by: Erkhyan Rafosa
Copy-editing by: Blarginator Bobcat

THE REWILDING

A STORY OF

MAMMALÆ ORIGINS

BY ERDBOK

WITH SPECIAL THANKS TO:

Suidpunt

Graypaw

ANNA

She knew winter was coming: Anna's coat had become thick, and she was hungry all the time. The air was cold, and there was fresh snow on the ground. There was movement in the tents by the clearing in the woods. Her ears perked up. A small creature scurried somewhere in the dark. The damp wood hissed and crackled in the flames. She smelled the last of their vegetables boiling in a pot. There was no danger for now.

A short while later, the rest of her tribe joined her by the fire where they all shared the soup. She licked every drop from her broken porcelain bowl. There were five foxes and four vixens—three fewer than winter before. Her tribe had aged. Only Anna and her half-sister, Katerina, were the right age to mate and have kits. She straightened the loose human t-shirt that covered her body to the knees. Anna felt it in her tummy when she saw Aleksandr look her way. He was a handsome fox who had joined them from another tribe. She wanted to be close to him, but he was usually in the woods. He wanted to impress Alexy—the strongest fox and the leader of the tribe—with his hunting skills.

Ivan was the other young fox. His eyes were always full of fear and his fur was rough. He would sometimes stare at Anna. She did her best to avoid him. The rest of the tribe was her father Nikolai, her mother Olga, her aunt Anya and their grandfather Viktor. Anna knew that Viktor would not live to the end of winter. Food was scarce. Sometimes the foxes came across unfriendly wolf-

or bear-tribes in the woods, but their biggest fear was humans. Sometimes, her tribe would find ruins filled with all sorts of old human junk. Mostly bits of metal and other broken things. If they were lucky, they found broken tools or old clothes. It felt like the humans tried to keep them alive, just so they could hurt them later. Man would leave the woods alone in summer and return to kill when it became cold. Their weapons ripped flesh from bone. Man hunted for the joy of killing and not for food. The elders often told them scary stories of how entire families of foxes were wiped out, their bodies left to harden in the snow. They might soon have to face man again as their supplies had run out and their prey had learned to avoid their hunting paths. They had to move.

The full moon hung between the stars in the cloudless sky. In her tent, Anna prepared for the journey. She filled the deer stomach with melted snow and wrapped the jerky and dried vegetables in a pouch. She made sure her two knives were sharp. One of them was for hunting—she kept it in a sling across her chest. The other was for skinning and dressing—she kept it with all her other things in an old human backpack. When Anna was happy with her preparation, she curled on her small mat with her bushy tail covering the tip of her nose. The fire went cold outside as she drifted off to sleep.

Her tribe walked for about a day when they decided to put up their tents again. Alexy had built a fire earlier in the day, and a black pot bubbled over it. The smell of roots and mushrooms made Anna's mouth water. Ivan and Alexy were in the woods; it was their turn to hunt. They hoped they could find some meat for their stew.

Anna sat by the fire with her arms wrapped around her knees. Her coat had fluffed out to keep her warm. She tried to make eye contact with Aleksandr who sat on the opposite side of the fire. He looked at her every now and then and smiled. She decided that it was time. Anna stood up and carefully walked towards him. Her tail swished from side to side. He looked up at her and smiled. Anna felt it in her tummy again.

She was about to sit down beside him when they heard a cry from the woods. Aleksandr leapt up. Anna pulled out her knife. Ivan had found something. He came from the trees, stopped, and tried to catch his breath. "Come! Look!"

The foxes left their camp and followed him. They climbed over fallen trees and waded through thick pockets of snow. They followed his tracks until he came to a sudden stop. He pointed. Anna and the others now stood beside him. They gasped. *"Could it be?"* In the shallow snow lay the body of a human. It wore a thick, olive-colored jacket and an *ushanka* over its head. He lay on top of—what appeared to be—his weapon.

Ivan sniffed. He tip-toed closer and went down on his knees. He touched the human's neck. "He is cold," he said. "He is alive, but his heart is slow." There was a strange thing stuck in his shoulder. Ivan pulled it out and looked at it. It was a small glass tube with a tail and a sharp needle at the tip. He threw it away. The man would surely die of cold, but the foxes decided not to touch him anymore: they would leave him to die. They could come back later to take his clothes, his weapon, and anything else that he had with him. The tribe was on edge. Another human did this. There must be another—or others—in the area.

The woods were deathly silent. Anna felt a shiver running up her spine, and her hackles stood on end. There was a pop. The tribe scattered in all directions and Anna felt a stinging pain in her neck. She yipped and leapt. Something fell from her. She tried to reach for her knife, but her paws and arms were weak. She fell in the snow. Even as she panicked, her heart rate slowed down and her skin felt cold. *"Poluchil yeye,"* she heard someone say.

Anna's eyes shot open. She wanted to scream, but there was not enough breath in her. There was a red glow around her. She saw the bars of a cage, and she was locked inside. The air was stale and stank of pee. Her own pee. She felt something sharp stuck in her shaved forearm, and there was a thick tube in her vixen bits. She wanted to tug them out, but her paws were bound together with a tight bandage. Her feet and knees were bound as well. There were wires stuck on her chest and a band around her digits. Anna's heart started pounding. It sent painful cramps up her chest. She made a few tiny yips, those of a tiny animal faced with cruel and certain death. There were strange sounds. Some kind of whirr. She felt her heart rate slow again and she felt nauseous. Her eyes closed. Anna's mind blacked out, but she was still in that dark, claustrophobic hell place in her dreams. They tormented her until she woke up again.

Anna woke up slowly and felt extremely confused. She remembered a forest in the snow. A dying man. A nightmare. She opened her eyes but saw only black. When she tried to sit, she bumped her head against the bars of a cage. Her body tensed. She lifted her head as far as she could, lowered her ears, and sniffed anxiously. The air around her was warm and dry. She scented another body, but it was faint. There were other smells too. There were cool patches on her body. The top of her paw was sore, and her vixen bits felt swollen. Anna's hackles rose. *"Gde ya?"* she whimpered and waited for a reply. *"Privet?!"* Still nothing. Terrified. She lay down again and reluctantly closed her eyes. *"A nightmare,"* she told herself, *"I will wake up soon."*

A New Place

Daylight fell over the vixen's brow. She slowly opened her eyes. The hot morning sun baked through the wide-open door. Isidore saw her wake. He set down his tablet, lifted his elbows from his knees, and straightened his back. He looked at her and smiled.

The vixen's eyes shot open. She yipped when she saw him. She snarled at him and bared her tiny canines. When he didn't show fear or retreat, she pulled back. The vixen made herself small in the very back of the cage and started shaking. "I not hurt you," he assured in very broken Russian as he raised his hand before him. He took his tablet from the floor, tapped a few commands, and raised it at her. On the screen was a mess of black shapes and blocks. Her terrified eyes scanned them. She immediately relaxed. "Smell," he commanded, holding his hand out towards her. He held it close enough for her to get a good sniff but far enough to protect him from her canines.

She crawled forward carefully. The vixen sniffed at his hand through the bars and then looked up at him. Puzzled. Her pupils dilated. "Yellow," she said in Russian.

Isidore carefully reached out and unlocked the cage. "You come out," he said.

She slowly crawled out the open gate, stretched. Trying to stand up, she nearly collapsed. She had no idea how long it'd been since she last used her arms and legs. He sized her up. The snow-white vixen had a young face with deep brown eyes and a tiny, black nose. She was about two heads shorter than him, and her build was skinny. Her posture was perfect for hunting. Clearly starved, she hardly had any breasts.

The vixen must have seen him look at her. She quickly tried to cover her nether regions with her paws and her tail. Isidore felt warm behind his ears. He reached for the floor beside him and picked up a large paper bag. He removed two folded garments and handed them to her. "You wear these," he said. She glanced suspiciously at the clothes as she unfolded them. The first was a light, white, short-sleeved t-shirt. Her tail twitched as she felt its gentle texture in her paw. She reluctantly pulled it over her head. It was a snug fit. The next item was a heavy, grey, one-piece overall that had no arms. It had stubby legs and a special slot for her tail. She struggled to put it on. Isidore was scared to approach her at first, but after a couple of minutes of seeing her frustration, he stepped up and helped her fasten the straps over her shoulders. She stretched her back and neck again.

He took his tablet, swiped his finger across the screen, and showed her a different mess of patterns and shapes.

"4725120453235319RM" she said.

He nodded, tapped on his device and showed it to her one last time.

"Green," she said.

"What is your name?" he asked. He now spoke MammalBasic, which was second nature to him. It was a simple language that was part of the Mammalæ BIOS. Her kind were born to understand it. It just needed to be activated by them seeing a simple semaphore. Isidore tapped on his device a few more times and looked up at her, waiting for an answer.

"I am Anna," she said. The vixen appeared spooked by the new language she suddenly spoke and the way the new words just rolled off her tongue.

"Is that your only name?"

"I have another name," she said, but the question appeared to make her feel *very* uncomfortable. "It... is my close name," she said. "Only my family can know it."

"I need *all* your names to for my records," said Isidore impatiently.

Anna swallowed hard. "They... call me Swiftpaw."

"Okay," he said. "I shall call you Anna, then. My name is Isidore, but you will call me master."

Anna nodded. "I am hungry and thirsty, m-master," she said.

"Come." He beckoned her to follow with his hand.

The small room opened into a larger space. She paused in the door to look around. Isidore's home was a cookie-cutter, mid-21st century, government subsidized apartment. There was a modestly sized television on the wall to the left of the living area and a big window to the far side of the living space, facing the rising sun. The floor was covered in worn, faux wood tiles. To the right, there was a small kitchen, separated from the living room by a wooden table and barstools. The kitchen was fitted out in more false wood. There were spartan appliances and a double basin. Leading out from the living area were three dark doors at the end of a short, featureless passage. There were several downlights along the ceiling. Some of them didn't work.

"Take a seat," he told Anna, pointing at one of the stools by the kitchen table. She carefully tucked her tail under her and sat down. The chair was human-approportionate, and she seemed to sit very uncomfortably. Her hind paws did not touch the ground. "Here is some food," he said as he leaned down and opened a cupboard. He pulled out a large, scrunchy bag and ripped it open. It smelled of bonemeal and something that vaguely resembled meat and vegetables. He poured a cup-full of the dry pellets into a bowl and pushed it towards her. Anna glared at it with a tilted head. He then filled a tall glass with water from the basin. He placed this before her too. Her eyes were immediately drawn to the clear liquid.

"I cannot drink from that," she said and pointed. He was puzzled for a moment, but then realized what she meant. Her pointy muzzle would make drinking from a glass very difficult. He nodded, reached into the cupboard again and took out a deep glass bowl. He filled it to the brim with water and placed it on the table before her.

"This is the best I can give you, for now."

Anna leaned forward, placed her nose close to the surface of the water, and started licking. When her thirst was quenched, she awkwardly dug into the pellets with her paw and stuffed some of them into her maw. She seemed to like the taste and continued eating until she was full. He left her by the table and returned to his study.

Anna climbed down from the stool and looked around the strange, new place again. The smell of chemicals irritated her sensitive nose. There was also the smell of dirty clothes and some kind of fruit.

She walked towards the large window. The outside looked more and more strange the closer she came. It was as high as the ceiling, but she could not see the ground. Or the sky. All she saw was a very tall structure across a wide gap. It was grey and lifeless. There were tiny black spots that ran up and down its side. She pressed her face against the glass, leaving a tiny wet mark with her nose. Anna looked down as far as she could, but she still saw the same. She realized that they were far above the ground. It made her feel sick. She turned away.

The panel against the wall that was dark before now showed a moving picture of a green forest, and it made gentle insect and nature sounds. She sniffed, but there was nothing. Anna immediately knew it was fake. There were some comfortable-looking bags on the floor. She tucked her tail between her legs and sat down on one. She stared blankly at the forest for a while.

Anna felt a very faint rush of air from an opening against the roof, and there was a tapping sound from down the passage. After a while she felt brave enough to look around. The short passage had three doors each with a room behind it. The first to the right was moist. It smelled of pee and mold.

There was a glass box, a strange porcelain seat, and something that looked like a fountain. *"This must be the latrine,"* she decided.

On the opposite side of the passage was a room like the one she woke up in. The scent of her master was very strong there, and she decided that it was where he slept. It was also the place where the dirty clothes smell came from. There were empty cupboards. All his clothes were on the floor and on his bed. There was only one small window from which she could see the same as from the one in the open area.

The tapping noises were loud now. Anna stepped to the door at the end of the passage. The fruity smell came from there, too. She stood in the doorway and saw her master leaning forward in a deep, worn-out chair. He was a stocky, middle-aged human. His eyes were serious. His back was slightly hunched. He had a small patch of fur below his bottom lip but not a single strand on his head. He didn't look very strong. His skin was darker than the humans she had seen before. He wore a loose shirt and short pants. His arms and legs were covered with fine brown fuzz.

There were five glowing panels in front of him. Three of them were on the kidney-shaped desk, and two were against the wall. There were several slabs of keys. Anna had only seen broken ones before. She had no idea what they did, but her master's hands moved over them very fast. There was a clicking sound every time he pressed one down. A bright green can stood on the desk next to him, and there were more piled up in a bin beside him on the floor. Anna sniffed. *"That must be where the awful smell comes from,"* she thought. On the other side of him was a rack full of machines with many, many tiny glowing lights. They flickered like tiny blinking eyes.

The room behind her master's back had shelves on every wall. All were full of strange-looking things. There were cables that hung all the way to the floor and stacks of paper. Books.

Anna looked at him again. Some of the panels moved with strange glowing symbols. She watched in awe. "Don't touch anything in here," he said without looking up. His tapping continued. Anna stood silently. Her master only took a short break every now and then to take a drink from the bright green can. *"How could he drink that stuff?"* she wondered.

"What is this?" she asked, pointing at the ceiling.

"This is my study," he said. "You are not allowed in here unless I specifically ask you to come." Anna nodded and turned back to the passage with her tail between her legs. "If you are bored," he called after her, "ask the television to show you something."

"Television?" she asked.

"That big panel on the wall," he said. "The thing showing the forest. Talk to it. Tell it what you want. You can speak Russian or MammalBasic. It will understand you and do what you tell it to. I'll see you later. I've got some work to do."

Back in the living area now, Anna was scared to talk to a non-living thing. She sat down before it several times and stared at the silent forest. Got up. Walked to the window and looked outside. Went back again. She thought about her tribe. Her people. *"What were they doing?"* she wondered. *"Where did they think she was? Did they think she was dead?"* It might be easier to explain that she died than to tell them where she was.

The day passed very, very slowly. Anna only saw her master twice, once after an *accident* in the latrine and once again when he gave her more food. It was the same food as in the morning. Early evening, she started to feel tired. Anna took a last look out the window. It was getting dark. Hundreds of tiny spots glowed across the gap. It made her feel sick again. She stepped away, turned, and headed back to her room. Her body ached and she felt sad. The lights were already off. She closed the door, made herself a bed, and lay down. *"I will wake up in the snow tomorrow,"* she thought as she closed her eyes.

Isidore opened his video surveillance app and tapped into the feed from her bedroom. In false color, he saw her sleep. Her bed was empty. Instead, she had thrown her duvet on the floor and curled up on top of it. Her overalls lay bundled on the floor beside her. She slept only in her shirt. For good measure, he checked the living room and the landing outside his door as well. As he expected—and as he had hoped—there was no one there. He closed the feed. Her day was over, but he was only getting started. There was an incoming comms.

USC Corporate
"Answer."

His main display—the largest one on the desk right in front of him—swept across a large boardroom with eight people seated around a stately table. A smartly dressed woman in grey and white sat at the head. She was skinny. Her face was flawless, and her frame was upright. Her green eyes were narrow and alert. She had a presence about her that even Isidore felt several tens of thousands of kilometers away. Along the sides of the table sat male and female subordinates. They were dressed similarly to her, but clearly, she was in charge. She looked straight at the camera while the others fiddled with their tablets on the table before them.

"Morning, Michelle," Isidore said.

"Hello, Robert. Did the specimen arrive?" She spoke in a moderate Bostonian accent.

"Yes, she did," he replied. "She came in last night. She's still very confused but she looks healthy. I'm sure she's suitable."

"We'd hope so," Michelle replied. "She's cost a lot of money."

"I won't disappoint you, ma'am."

Michelle nodded. "Are there any questions from the table?" The camera followed her gaze. A man with glasses raised his hand. "What does her serial number tell us?"

"Give me a moment," Isidore said, tapping a few keys on one of his keyboards. "I ran the numbers. I can confirm this:

```
Naturally Conceived Mammal, 14th Generation
Species Vulpus Lagopus Anomalis (Mammalæous)
Serial Number 4725120453235319RM
MæOS 1.3.0.2.0000015
Type Research
```

He looked up at his audience again. A woman raised her hand. "What's her age?"

"I can't confirm it at this time," he said, "but I will have an answer at our next meeting. She looks young."

"How's the MæSIM doing?" asked another.

"It is running well. I've extracted every bit of data I can from it. The decompilation process is at about fifty-four percent. The rest of the code will come as the specimen starts interacting with it."

"Do you know what *her* processing power is?"

"I don't have a benchmark for her," replied Isidore, "But honestly? I don't think it matters."

"What do you mean?"

"Like a great company once said—the power is *adequate*."

"I still don't get what you are saying. I don't think it's a stupid question?"

"There was a moment in time," explained Isidore, "when engineers realized that silicon wafers weren't the only way to create a computer. Computers can be grown. Transistors per square millimeter. Cores and petaflops aren't the only criteria to determine how useful a machine is." He smiled. "SFA corporation realized this very early on. No offense. I think your company chose to go all-out in the complete opposite direction—but that's your business," he was quick to add.

"Anything else?" Michelle asked. There was silence. "Very well. We'll talk to you again soon." The comms ended. There was already another on hold.

Rick
"Answer."

On the monitor before him was a mint-green anthropomorphic fox, shown from the shoulders up. He wore a casual shirt with the top button undone. He had a bright smile across his fluffy face and a twinkle in his eyes. "Hey buddy!" he greeted.

"Rick," said Isidore, "...or should I say, the *one and only* GreenFox958202?"

His friend feigned offense. "Oh, that's rich coming from *Saint Isidore of Seville—Patron saint of computers, their users, programmers, repair people as well as the entire friggin' Internet!*"

"Yeah, yeah, whatever."

With a tap of Rick's hand-paw the avatar disappeared. In its place sat a balding man with a neckbeard and a chubby face.

"How are things on your end?" asked Isidore.

"Never mind how things are *here*... Talk to *me* Saint! Is she there? What's she like? Will you send me a picture?"

"Yes, she's here," Isidore said with a sigh. "She's sleeping right now. I promise I'll send you a picture tomorrow. Everything's okay. She was completely zoned out. Wandered up and down all day between her room, the television, the window, and her pellets on the kitchen table." Isidore paused. "I knew she was wild, but I had no idea. I'm still trying to get the stench out of my apartment."

"Does she smell?"

"Her coat is okay," Isidore replied, "It's not the worst I've smelled—as far as Mammalæ go anyway. But, um—she had an *accident* earlier. She didn't know what to do in the bathroom, so she took a dump in the shower."

Rick's lips curled. "That's... gross!"

"She didn't know any better." Isidore shrugged. "She felt bad about it and was very embarrassed. I had to explain to her how to use the toilet. That was very awkward. To get the *debris* down the shower drain nearly made me puke."

"When are you taking her to Cath?"

"Tomorrow," Isidore said. "We're going there early."

"Ok, well... best of luck, Saint! I hope everything goes well."

"Keep well buddy. I'll let you know how it goes." Isidore cracked open another Blast and started re-reading the script he had written. Scrolling along hundreds of lines of text, it took him about half an hour to find his rhythm again. Another comms came in.

Yuri

"Leave me alone!" he thought. "Answer."

The man on the other side had a hard face, bright blue eyes, and a beanie over his wide brow. "Yuri," Isidore said, "yes, she came in this morning. And yes, she's alive."

"Good," he said in a very thick Slavic accent. "When I get paid?"

"I told you. You need to talk to USC. They said they'll pay as soon as the work is done. Maybe it will take a day or two to reflect in your account?"

"*Bud'-yakyy chas,*" he said proudly. "I give it another day." The screen went dark.

Isidore re-re-read the code. This time it took him nearly an hour to start writing new lines. Another call came in.

Unknown Party
"Reject call."

Isidore bent forward and bumped his head on his desk a couple of times. *"This is fucking ridiculous. That's it. I'm done."*

ONLINE

Anna was sad when she woke up in the same space as the day before, but the room felt lighter. Her scent clung to the duvet and her clothes. She felt the warm morning sun.

Her master was at the kitchen table with a bowl of food in front of him. He did not touch the spoon—he was too busy tapping and sliding his finger across his device. *"What are those things?"* Anna wondered.

"Hello Anna," he said.

"Hello master." She remembered what he did the day before. Anna went to the kitchen cupboard and reached for the bag of pellets.

"You can't eat anything this morning," he said.

"Why?" she asked with a tiny frown.

"I'm taking you to the doctors, and she asked that you must wait 'til after she sees you. To eat something."

Anna frowned. "A doctors?"

"You'd probably call them *healers* back where you are from."

Anna nodded. She sat with a watering maw by the table, watching her master eat a bland-smelling paste. He still tapped his device. "What is that?" she asked. He looked puzzled, as if he did not understand what she meant. Anna pointed at his device.

"These things? They are called *tablets*. Or *pads*. They let us see things that are happening in the world. We can use them to talk to other people very far away. Do shopping. Do all kinds of things."

Anna was only slightly less confused. She got up and stood by the window for a while. Then she realized something: even though she had only been there a day, she had not seen or heard another human. Or any mammalæ. It was probably a stupid question, but she could not keep it inside. "Where is your tribe?" she asked, "who is your leader?"

Her master looked up from his tablet again. "Our world is very, very different from yours," he said. "It's impossible for me to explain it to you." He saw her disappointment and tried to give her some things to think about. "Yes, we humans have leaders. They are far away. We never get to see them, apart from on our screens. We have parents and friends, but there are no tribes here. We don't live together." He shrugged. "In this world, everyone does exactly what they want. Only the law says what you cannot do. And there's also *money* that holds everything together. You probably haven't heard of money either."

Anna's ears felt warm. "I am sorry that I have so many questions, master."

"Things will make more sense in time," he said. "Just watch and learn—and trust," he was quick to add.

"Can I ask you a different question?"

"Yes, you can."

"Why am I here?"

He thought before answering. "I brought you here to help me. Exactly how is also very hard to explain. But I promise I will take good care of you—this is a dangerous place," he added. "You must not leave me at any time. Which reminds me. I still need to register your chip."

"Chip?"

Isidore showed the top of his left hand to her. "Every one of us has a small thing in our left hand or paw. It lets us move around. It also allows us to pay for things."

Anna touched the top of her left paw and felt a tiny bump. She shivered. *"How did it get there?"* she wondered. The more he spoke, the less everything made sense! *"You'll see."* and *"It's hard to explain."* were the answers to nearly all the things she asked.

"We'll be going out soon," he said, "but first come with me." They went to his study. Her master tapped away at one of his keyboards, then took a small machine from a drawer. Anna recognized the shape as that of a human weapon. She tensed up, but he gestured for her to stay calm. "When you see one of these," he said, "show your left paw. Like this," he gestured with his hand. She did. Very reluctantly. When the device touched, it made a beep sound. Her arm twitched. The back of the machine lit up and showed some glowing symbols. "Great," he said. He rode his chair back under his desk and tapped some more. "You are now registered on the city's database," he said. "What a pathetic excuse for access control. Easy as pie!"

The sun had risen. Its yellow light was warm without making shadows. Anna sat in the living area and stared at the television. It showed a place by the big waters with soft yellow sand and tall, slender trees. There was the sound of water. She was incredibly frustrated that she was not allowed to eat. Her mouth watered all the time.

She heard soft conversation from the passage. Her master seemed to be talking to himself, and he spoke a language she did not understand. She heard him get up from his chair.

"Let's go." He took his tablet and gestured for her to follow him. They went to the only door she had not seen open yet. He touched a small panel. There was a clack, and he pulled it open. There was a slight gust of air. Many new smells flowed in. "Follow me."

The smell of food was strong. Anna's mouth water even more. The passage was long, its walls and ceilings pale green. The grey floor felt sticky beneath her paws. There were windows to their right and many doors to their left. Anna sniffed. "Come," he kept saying.

She looked around her. *"I need to find something, in case I need to run,"* she thought. But she knew she would not. She was too scared. She already felt lost.

Air flowed in from holes in the ceiling, and there were also long glowing tubes that made light. The windows stopped, and there was another set of doors. They were shiny. Her master reached out and tapped a small pad between them. An orange symbol appeared. *"Everything has a panel,"* Anna thought. They waited for a few counts, then the doors opened and there was a small space. Anna reluctantly followed him inside. The doors closed, and he pressed another button. There was a strange feeling in her tummy and a very soft rumble. Ding! The doors slid open again, but they were now in a different place altogether. Again.

Anna's shoulders tensed up. It was not a passage, but a big open space. It had dark stone floors and brown brick walls. Bright light came from a wide entrance at the far end. There was a row of uncomfortable-looking seats against the wall on the right, and there were three large televisions on the left. They showed glowing symbols that meant nothing to her. Another human walked past them. He was talking with an angry voice to someone she could not see. He did not greet. It became hotter as they walked to the light. They stopped by a mammal sitting at a wooden table by the door. He was some kind of dog. He sat on a worn-out, uncomfortable-looking human chair. There was a tablet on his lap. His clothes were like hers, but the overalls were black instead of grey.

He looked up at her master and nodded. "Take her smell," he instructed, pointing to her.

"She is my new mammal. She will be staying with me."

The dog nodded again. He slowly stood up and looked her over. He gestured for her to give him her paw, which she did reluctantly. He sniffed and said something in her master's language. He looked her in the eyes. "Welcome ma'am," he said, now in MammalBasic. "I hope you enjoy your new home."

Anna held her breath as they stepped outside. The heat hit her like a stone wall to the side of the muzzle. For a moment, she was too stunned to move. It felt like her coat was on fire! Even the air she breathed was hot and dry. It took her a moment to open her eyes completely. She stood still and was dumbstruck by what she saw.

She looked left.

She looked right.

They were in a place between two enormous buildings. She could not see the sky. There were two wide black roads with a narrow island in the middle. The roads were very smooth and flat, and there were two shiny stripes along their middle. Above the roads were cables. There were poles with bright red, orange, and green lights. Humans and mammalæ walked on both sides. Most of them were looking at their tablets, but there were some who looked like they were talking to real, other people. Others just walked along. Her hind paws felt very hot.

Anna sniffed. There was the scents of other bodies and the smell of tar—and food.

"Come. Stay close!" Anna was happy when they could walk in the shadows. There were lines of rectangular, four-wheeled and clusters of narrow, two-wheeled things at each side of the road. Anna jolted the first time she saw one move. She nearly leapt into the road the first time she heard one make a loud barking sound.

There was a bell. An even larger thing rolled along the metal strips. She saw it stop. Humans and mammalæ got out and others got back in. Her tail was between her legs. There were dead trees inside large square holes every few paces. She sweated and panted. Her watery eyes wanted to close all the time.

She had only ever seen bear and wolf tribes in her life, but she knew there were other kinds of mammalæ, too. She did not think that there were so many! A feline in white overalls pushed an elderly human across the path in a chair with wheels. A buck with spiral horns poured water on the foot of one of the dead trees.

They came to a set of lights. Her master touched a panel and waited. The vehicles rolling down the road stopped. The red light turned green. They crossed. The black surface was coarse and unbearably hot. Her paws still burned as they stepped under a large, covered walkway and went inside a cool building. They were in a crowded place, and there was a rotten, musty smell. It was the smell of paws and feet. Humans and mammalæ moved around, some in lines in front of tall, strange-looking machines. Others watched some of the many television screens.

She followed her master to a line of posts that separated the area into two. There were gates between them that slid open to let people through, one at a time. He glanced at her to make sure she was watching what he did. He held the back of his left hand to a round yellow panel on the front of the post. It beeped. The dividers opened and closed again after he had walked through. He looked back. "Do the same," he said above the noise. "Your pass is already loaded."

Anna did. There was a beep, a click, and the gate opened. Anna stepped through, carefully not to have the gate close on her tail. They walked down a long set of stairs and came to a long, tunnel place. The air around them moved. There was now a new smell—that of grease—and another chemical she had not smelled before. Anna nearly lost sight of her master in the crowd. There was a long, narrow platform with a dark lowered part behind a long yellow line. There were two dark tunnels, one on each side. Everyone stood waiting. *"What are we waiting for?"* she wondered. She looked at her master. He did not look back. There was a ding-dong sound, and an invisible voice said something. A sudden gust of wind and a loud rumble and a giant worm-like machine burst from the tunnel and slowed into their space. It stopped with a bone-chilling screech. Anna's heart raced, and she had to fight the urge to run. Several doors opened. Humans and mammalæ got out onto the platform and others got back in. She and her master stepped aboard.

 The scents of other bodies were so overwhelming that she stopped trying to pick them apart. The doors closed by themselves. There was a tug, and the space around them started moving. Anna grabbed a metal bar to stay upright. After a few moments she got used to the strange feeling of moving forward without walking. She looked around her. There were many other mammalæ. Sheep, rodents, dogs. Many humans, too. She was surprised that no-one looked at her. Many of the others were doing things on their tablets. They did not seem to care about the movement around them at all. The other mammalæ wore more-or-less the same clothes she did, white shirts and full-body overalls. The only difference was the colors: most were blue, red, black, or white. The humans all wore different clothes. Most of them wore loose shirts and short pants made of a soft material. Some of their shirts were decorated with letters and symbols. A group of women wore clothes that covered everything except their eyes and hands. They stood at the side of the worm and seemed scared of another woman who leaned against the opposite side. She chewed something that wasn't food. Her teats were uncovered. She looked like she didn't even care. Anna shivered. Some humans had light skins—like her master. Others had darker skins. Some had straight fur on their heads. Some had curls, and some had no fur at all. She never knew there were so many kinds of humans!

The worm rumbled and shook. Every now and then, it made a bone-chilling grind. Anna looked at her master. He stared ahead, and his face did not show any feeling. There were a thousand questions in her mind. "Where are we going?" she asked again.

"I already told you, we're going to the doctor's," he said. He seemed annoyed. She looked away from him and didn't ask any more questions. She was scared. There was nothing wrong with her, and she couldn't imagine why she would need to see a healer. Fourteen seasons old, she had never been to one; the last healer in their tribe died before she was born. Anna did the same as her master and stared at the darkness outside. *"Perhaps,"* she thought, *"there was something in the dark he saw, that I did not?"*

The machine stopped and took off again, four times. Then they stepped out, went through another set of sliding gates, climbed up a staircase, and went back outside. It was a different place, but it looked the same as before: tall buildings, dark roads, and terrible heat. They took a walk. Just as they were about to turn into a smaller road between two buildings, they were stopped by two humans in brown uniforms and caps. One was male and the other was female. Their uniforms made them look important. *"And,"* Anna thought to herself, *"sweltering."* The male greeted them in his own language. He looked at Anna.

Her master seemed uneasy. He showed his upturned hand. They held a device against it, and there was a beep. The man examined the readout. Anna heard them say, "Robert." A short conversation followed. The man then asked something, looking at Anna. Her master looked at her and nodded. She was terrified with everyone looking at her. She was scared of what they were saying about her.

The woman stepped forward and gestured for Anna to show her paw. She did. Beep. "Anna." She recognized her name but did not know what else the woman said. Anna withdrew her paw. The man and woman in brown seemed happy and let them go.

Vehicles rolled by. Bodies milled. Anna was relieved when they stepped into a cool building. The doors were wide and open. It had a gentle smell that Anna liked. A cat with brown, white, and black fur sat behind a box-shaped desk in the middle of a wide, clean passage. There was a panel with glowing red lights on the wall behind her and two sliding gates beside. Pictures on the walls showed happy mammalæ doing fun things with their masters. Her own master greeted and spoke to the feline, who casually said something in return. Anna heard her name again. He nodded and held out his hand and gestured for her to do the same. They were both beeped.

Anna followed her master into one of the small moving spaces. The doors opened. They walked down another passage and into a large clean-smelling room with smooth white floors. A goat in white overalls pushed a dog in blue overalls along in a wheeled chair. The dog had metal parts sticking from his left leg. He did not seem to be in pain, but it still made Anna's mane stand on end. At the far side of the room, there was a desk with a clever-looking rat behind a sheet of glass. He nodded as they entered. The man spoke to him. She recognized her name again. The rodent continued to tap away at his tablet as they took a seat. The chairs were comfortable. Some were made for humans and other ones had gaps for tails.

In the corner of the room there were two small televisions. One showed humans talking to one another and the other showed several pieces of unmoving information with red-, green-, and yellow-colored blocks next to them. Anna rubbed her sore hind paws together. There were more pictures against the walls here, but they were different. The pictures showed mammalæ with injuries, being taken care of by friendly humans in white clothes. They were in a place her kind came when they were hurt, but it looked a lot different from what she thought a healer's place would look like. She was not like the dog in the wheeled chair. She was not like any of the pictures that she saw. She was not sick! Anna tried to calm herself by staring at the television. Her tail twitched.

After a short wait, the rat touched his panel, slid and dragged his claw along its surface. "Robert?" he asked as he looked up. The man stood up and the rat said some things. Her master nodded. A strange, scaled creature with a long snout came to fetch them. She led them down a long, wide passage where they entered a bright space. It had beds against the walls, with a wide-open passage between them. Some of the beds were closed off with big white curtains. There were also strange machines with pipes and wires. Two humans in white—the kind she saw on the posters—stood behind a large desk. They nodded at her master and her before they carried on talking. The scaled creature took Anna to an empty bed and asked her in MammalBasic to sit down on top of it. She drew curtains around them. Her master took a seat in a chair beside the bed. He scratched his head and looked up at the ceiling.

Nothing happened for a few minutes. They did not speak. All Anna heard was the occasional beep and the rush of air. She was more scared than ever.

Anna jolted as the curtains around them parted. A human female dressed in loose-fitting green clothes stepped in. She was tall and healthy-looking. She had a warm, motherly face. There were strands of yellow hair that stuck from under a blue cap on her head. She had some kind of mask around her neck. "Hello Anna," she said with a friendly smile—and in the language Anna understood. She leaned forward to bring her head in line with Anna's. She held out her hand. Anna instinctively leaned forward and sniffed. The woman's scent was friendly. It was not mixed with chemicals like that of her master. She immediately liked her. "Hello Isidore," she said, then turned back to Anna. "I am Doctor Catherine. I will be taking care of you.

"Isidore, will you please leave us?" He stood up and left. The doctor checked to make sure the curtains were completely closed. She then spoke softly. "Don't be scared, Anna. If I do anything that makes you feel uncomfortable, just say so and I will stop." Anna nodded. "Now, Anna, I want to check if you are healthy. And to do that, I am going to have to touch you with my hands. Are you okay with that?" Anna nodded nervously. The healer put on some stretchy white gloves and covered her mouth and nose with the mask. "Please open your maw so I can look at your teeth." Anna opened her muzzle. The healer took a small light and folded Anna's lips over her gums and gently looked around. "A little bit of plaque," she said, "nothing to worry about."

"Now Anna, will you please roll down your overalls to your lap, so I can listen to your heart and lungs?" The healer's caring voice made her calm. Her chest and back felt cool as the top of her overalls fell onto her lap. The healer placed a cool thing on her chest, then on her back. "Breathe in. Breathe out." She did a couple of other things that Anna didn't understand. But she worked with the healer and did everything she asked. "Very good," the healer said. "Have you had anything to eat this morning?" Anna shook her head. "Have you been to the toilet today?" Anna nodded. "Good," the healer said with a smile. "How are you feeling Anna? Is there anything hurting or making you uncomfortable? Your tummy? Your head?"

"My paws hurt," she said, raising her legs.

"Poor thing," the healer said, "I know it's hot out there. Don't worry, Anna. We'll make them feel better." Anna was skeptical but nodded. "Now, Anna, I'm going to go outside for a few minutes. I want you to remove your clothes completely and put this on." She handed her a light blue one-piece cloth. "When you are done, please lie down with you back on the bed, your tail tucked downwards. Rest your head on the pillow and try to relax."

Anna would not do it for any other human in the world. She was completely naked for a moment as her overalls dropped to the floor. She stuck her arms through the front-to-back garment. It was light, and it cooled her whole body. It felt good. She climbed back onto the narrow bed and took another careful look around her. Then she lay down her head and stared at the ceiling. The healer came back a few moments later.

Anna had no idea what would happen next. The healer took a tablet from the table behind her. "I want you to look at this," she said. A mess of black on white patterns danced before Anna's eyes. They seemed... familiar. She suddenly felt dizzy, and there was a tickly sensation in her paws. *So... peaceful...* Her eyes closed.

Catherine waited until she was sure Anna was fully anaesthetized before opening the curtains. The pangolin nurse that had been standing by approached. "Please prepare her for surgery," Catherine said.

"Yes doctor," the pangolin said, nodding. She raised the guardrails at the bed's sides, released the brakes, and pushed the bed away from its station and down the passage.

Catherine went back to the waiting room and summoned Isidore. They made their way along a maze of corridors until they came to her office. She sat down behind her desk. Her friendly demeanor had gone. He crossed his arms. "Just so you know," she started, "the only reason I agreed to do this *highly illegal* procedure is because I hate the corporation as much as you do. Not only is it *illegal*, but I also consider it highly *unethical*." She continued, "It's a delicate operation. There's only about a seventy percent chance she'll make a full recovery. If she doesn't, she'll have permanent and serious neurological damage. She could wake up to excruciating pain, and we'd have to put her down. Immediately. You might not see her again."

Isidore nodded without breaking eye contact. "That would be unfortunate, Cath. She's a good specimen."

Catherine felt the anger boil in her. "Have you even spoken to her about what you are doing to her, Robert?"

"Informed consent only applies to humans," he said. "She's an android who just happens to have a fleshy body and a fleshy computer for a brain. I even have the source code to prove it." He was quick to add, "Well, I have most of it."

Catherine was not impressed. "Anna is no more a fleshy android with a fleshy computer for a brain than you are. Lose the God complex, okay?" She sighed and got up from her chair. "I must go. I'll tab you when she's ready. Book an Autotaxi. She won't be able to walk on her own for at least a day or two."

Isidore was nearly out the door when Catherine spoke again. "Also, I will be wiping her memory as of midnight last night. She won't remember anything and will most likely think that you did this to her. If I were you, I'd start thinking of a good explanation of what you did. And why."

He nodded. "I'll let you carry on with your work."

Shawn

Anna woke up and felt sick. She was in her room. It felt like she had slept for days, but she was still tired. When she tried to sit, she immediately felt dizzy and lay down again. Her eyes were wide open, and she stared at the ceiling. There was a cold spot on her forearm, and there was something hard behind her ear. She reached out and touched it. It was slightly painful, so she left it alone. Her lips were dry. She needed to drink some water. "Master," she croaked and tried to sit again.

"Anna," he said, stumbling into the door. "How do you feel?"

"What happened?" she asked, "What is this behind my ear? I'm thirsty, but I cannot stand up! My legs are so weak!"

"Just keep calm," he said, gesturing with his hands. "I'll bring you some water." He ignored her question about the thing behind her ear, stepped out, and returned with a new, long-lipped cup that fit into her muzzle. She could drink from it. Anna gulped the water down and managed to get some water in her nose. She coughed and snorted. He stepped up and patted her back. She stretched her neck and then lay down again.

"What is this behind my ear?" she asked.

"It's um... a very special thing," he said. "It will help you learn new things very quickly. And it will let you experience new things. It's hard to explain, but um—you will see in the next few days or so. It is not dangerous. Just... don't tug or scratch it, ok?"

Anna touched the strange thing again. His explanation wasn't good—as always—but she agreed that she should not touch it or scratch the skin around it. It definitely went inside her skin, and it felt like it went deep inside her head. Her head felt swollen, and there was a ringing sound in her ears. "Are you hungry?" he asked.

"No."

"You should get some rest. Let me know if you need anything."

Anna spent the next two days in her room, only leaving to eat, drink, and visit the latrine. Her master gave her three white pills with every meal. The pain behind her ear was bad the first day but gradually became better. After three days it was gone.

Anna stood up and walked to the kitchen. She filled her cup and poured some pellets into her bowl.

"How are you feeling today?" asked her master as he stepped out of his study.

"I am feeling better now, master." There was an awkward moment of silence.

"I am going to show you some amazing things," he said. Her ears perked up. "When you are done eating, come back to your room." She nodded and continued to eat. He carried a piece of machinery from his study. It wasn't a tablet—it was a large, flat box with a smaller one on top of it. There were a few cables hanging from it. She heard him do things. After eating she got up, visited the latrine, and went back to her room to see what he was doing.

On a table beside her bed stood the machine. It had a long cable that was plugged into the wall. It had many lights, like the machines in his study. He sat on a chair with another strange device on his lap. It looked like a tablet, but it had a keyboard as well. He put it down and gestured for her to lay down on the bed. "Keep your arms by your side and point your tail downwards between your legs. Make yourself comfortable. This is perfectly safe and won't hurt."

Her heart thumped. *What was he going to do to her?*

"Look at this," he said, showing her a grid of patterns on his tablet. It seemed... familiar. In a moment all her fear was gone, and she went to sleep.

Isidore took a cable from the floor. It was the female counterpart of the uplink behind her ear. Her body twitched ever so slightly when it made first contact. He then picked up his portable and typed up some commands. He was elated when he saw her prompt flicker up on the terminal for the first time. The operation was successful.

He was inside her brain. She was receptive.

His heart raced. *"First things first,"* he thought, *"let's get to know you a bit better."* He kicked off a comprehensive diagnostics script and watched the lines on the terminal roll by. He saved the output and did a quick scan through. Her processor, memory, and secondary storage were in excellent condition. He would take a closer look at the rest of the logs that evening when she slept. He issued an eject command. When the connection closed and it was safe, he carefully unplugged her. A few minutes later, she opened her eyes. "What did that feel like?" he asked.

"I don't know what you mean," she said. "But I am thirsty." He offered her a cup of water.

"I have a big surprise for you tomorrow. You'll love it!" She tilted her head curiously. "But we'll continue tomorrow. You are probably exhausted. Your mind still needs some exercise before we can do longer sessions." Her eyes made it clear that she didn't have any idea what he was talking about. He helped her off the bed and parked her before the television. This time round, it was showing a rustic savannah with yellow grass, sparse green bushes, and thorn trees. The sound was that of rustling insects and the wind combing the grass. Anna dozed off a couple of times before finally retiring to her room.

Isidore checked her camera later that evening as she slept. She lay in her usual place on the floor. He smiled and closed the feed. He triumphantly snapped open a can of Blast. In a single swinging movement, he deposited the empty one into the overflowing trash can beside him. He stretched his back, letting out a groan. "What a day," he thought, and smiled. There was an incoming comms.

Rick
"Answer."

Hey Rick, you beat me to it. How are things?"
"I'm doing well Saint. How's Anna?"

"She survived the op. I linked her up for the first time today. Ran some diagnostics. Everything looks good."

"Oh, that's great! Have you hooked her up to the MæSIM yet?"

"Not yet. Her brain still needs to build a bit more stamina. She was completely exhausted after the diagnostics script. I will try to hook her up tomorrow."

"I forgot to ask last time," said Rick, "has she taken to you?"

"What do you mean?"

"Do you feel you are bonding with her?"

"You know how I feel about these creatures," said Isidore. "I'm a computer guy. They are computers. I think it's pointless to have any kind of relationship with them." He paused. "But if you want to know about imprinting—yes, that's done. But she gave me a yellow, not a green."

"Ok—what does that mean? Is that a bad thing?"

Isidore raised his hands. "This was before I had the comms port hooked up, so I don't know exactly what happened. Maybe the imprint semaphore returned some sort of warning? Perhaps because of her age? At least it wasn't red. Otherwise she'd be hostile towards me."

"She's wild-caught. Don't you think it could have anything to do with it?"

"Possibly," Isidore said. "Her tribe's been in isolation for many generations, nearly as long as Mammalæ have existed. She might have gotten a very old version of MæOS from her parents—one that responds differently to the modern deck." He glanced at one of his other displays for a moment. "Oh, and here," he said. "I took a picture of her."

Rick's face lit up. "Wow, she's pretty! You know," he continued as if suddenly stung by a grand idea. "You really, really, *really* should bring her to our next convention. Not many arctic foxes. Heck, not many foxes there. She'll be the star of the show!"

"I... don't know if that's a good idea. I want to keep her out of the public eye. I also don't think she's ready for a crowd," Isidore said, slightly annoyed. "But for interest's sake, when is your next convention?"

"This weekend!" Rick was chipper. "I've got a brand-new suit I'll be wearing for the first time, too!" he paused. "You must loosen up, buddy. You are working yourself sick."

"Sick? I'm feeling just fine." There was a pause in their conversation.

"Listen, I've got to check on some commissions. Keep well Saint! Sleep well if you do." The conversation ended. Isidore popped his knuckles and dove into creating more scripts.

He waited for Anna to wake up by herself the next day but wasted no time preparing her for another online session. After she had eaten, drank some water, and visited the bathroom, he instructed her to lie down again. He prepped her, put her to sleep, and hooked her up.

Anna lay on a patch of moist grass in the middle of a forest. She sat up, her heartbeat fast. She looked around. The smell was that of soil, rotting wood, and crushed leaves. The sun's light shone through the leaves of the trees and made bright spots on the grass. She pitched her ears. There was a breeze, and she heard water flowing in the distance. Anna rose to her hind paws and stretched her back. She was naked. Her neck fur had regrown, and the thing behind her ears was gone.

"*Did I die?*" she wondered. "Hello?" she called. "He-hello?" She waited. And waited.

There was no reply.

She stood for a while. Then she took a step into the woods. Anna moved in the direction of the water. Soon, she came to a stream where clear water flowed over moss-covered tree roots and rocks. The riverbed was filled with tiny pebbles. She could swear she saw a fish. Anna kneeled and tasted the water. It tasted wonderful. Clean. Not like the bitter water at her master's place. She stood there for a while, just listening. *"I should move upstream,"* she thought. *"If there are others here, that is what they would do."*

The plants were not thick, and in places, it looked like there was already a path. *"Am I alone?"* she wondered. Anna shuddered when she thought that there might be predators. It *felt* safe, but she could not be sure. She did not have her knife. She didn't even have clothes to protect her body. Anna knew she would be hungry soon. Without her knife, she could only kill small creatures like rabbits and birds. Or maybe she could find some fruit or mushrooms?

She stopped and sniffed. There was the faint smell of burning wood. *"A camp?"* she wondered as her heart began to beat fast again. She walked a bit farther. Then she saw it. Under a large, old tree, there was a small tent. Before it was a fire with a small black pot that hung from a frame. Her tail flicked. "Hello?" There still was no reply. She went closer and carefully looked into the tent. There was nobody inside, but there was a thick mat on the soil and some bags in the back. She was not comfortable digging through them. Not yet.

Her ears perked up. There was movement. She stumbled from the tent. Her body tensed and her hackles raised. From the shadows, she heard the crunching of branches and the rustling of grass. She raised her paws and arched her back, ready to leap. Or run. The steps became louder and louder. More rushed. A creature stepped out. It stopped dead in its tracks when it saw her. Anna gasped with her paw to her muzzle. It was another fox! As it stepped into the light, she could see him for the first time. He was a woodland fox with auburn fur and a big, bushy tail like her own. He was about her size. He was also naked. It was as if he had seen a ghost.

"Hello?" he whimpered.

Anna tried to cover her vixen bits with her tail. "Stay back!" she warned, but she didn't flee. He was too far to scent, but they stared at each other with maws slightly parted.

"My name is Shawn," he shouted with a smile. "Wow! I am so happy to see another fox! What is your name?" He seemed friendly.

"I am Anna," she said, lowering her paws slightly.

"I won't hurt you," he promised, with his paws raised to his shoulders.

"Where am I?" she asked.

"We're in a forest." He had a confused look on his face.

"I know that," she said. "What... where is the forest?" Anna's question seemed to confuse him even more.

"I... am not sure what you mean. It's a forest. And we are in it. Where did *you* come from?"

Anna sucked a canine and scratched the back of her head. *"This is strange,"* she thought. *"This does not make sense!"*

"Gosh, I'm happy to see another fox," he said again. "It's so quiet here. I'm cooking lunch. Do you want to join me?"

Anna nodded, still not fully trusting him. They sat down by the fire. He leaned over the pot and sniffed. Shawn scooped some soup into two small enamel bowls and gave one to Anna. She licked at the warm liquid without looking away from him.

Isidore watched their exchange from the console. To him, there was no forest. No water. No soup. Only a stream of code. For now, he could discern words—not sentences—though the patterns were structured. The raw data streamed simultaneously from the MæSIM emulator—that was Shawn—and from Anna's computer brain. It all funneled into the memory of his main processor in the study. It had already started crunching through the data. Isidore looked at Anna where she lay in suspended animation. Her eyelids twitched ever so slightly. Isidore knew he'd have to bring her back soon. He didn't want to overstretch her mind, but hopefully she had seen enough to want to go back. She was slow to respond to the eject command.

Anna was very confused. She sat up, opened her maw to speak, and found she could not. There was a tiny speck of blood on the pillow where her head was.

"You must be thirsty," said her master, as if nothing had happened.

Her mouth was dry. She sniffed the air and looked around. "What happened?" she asked. "Where was I?"

Her master did not respond, only smiled.

She stepped off the bed and paused for a moment. She sniffed and looked around her again. Anna followed him to the kitchen where a bowl of pellets and a cup of water awaited her. "Where... Where was I?" she mouthed through the chewing.

"You were in a forest," he said.

"I know that master," she said, annoyed. "How did I get there? Where is the forest? How—?"

"It's a special place," he said. "A place between the real world and the world of dreams, but," he was quick to add, "it's as real as you want it to be."

Anna bit her tongue. *"Wherever it was,"* she thought, *"it was better than this place."* She thought of Shawn, probably still in the forest. Alone. *"Did he see her go? What did he think of it all?"*

"Did you meet Shawn?" he asked, as if he could read her mind.

"Yes," she said, surprised. "Do you know him? He is friendly."

"I've spoken to him a couple of times. And yes, he is nice. You can visit him again tomorrow," he said. "I want you to rest now. Watch some TV. Or take a nap."

Twilight. Anna stood by the window again. Her master sat at the kitchen table, tapping and swiping away at his tablet with a bowl of noodles before him. She gazed at the flickering lights of the buildings across. "Can we go outside?" she asked.

He looked up from his tablet and frowned. He thought for a moment, then nodded. "Ok," he said, "I'm not leaving the building this time of night, but I guess we can go to the roof. Come."

The rooftop was high, but there were other rooftops that were even higher. The air smelled of soot but was cool and pleasant. The land was nearly dark. There were tiny lights as far as she could see—there were more than there were stars in the sky. Anna had never seen such a thing before, but she grabbed her muzzle and gasped as she looked behind her. Above the glowing lights of more buildings and the dark side of a great black mountain, there were fluffy pink and bright orange clouds in a deep purple sky. Anna had only ever seen the dancing green lights before. This was something new. It was one of the most beautiful things she had ever seen.

She reached out with her paw, as if to touch it. She shut her eyes, took a deep breath, and lowered her paw as she opened her eyes again. She looked at her master. "Is this how high we can go?" she asked as the wind rustled her fur. Her master nodded. She looked at the sky again. The colors were now nearly gone, and the clouds were turning grey. "Thank you master," she said, "I feel better now."

Isidore—wired on energy drinks—pored over the data they had produced during the simulation. It would take him a while to get a grip on things, but his computers never rested. There was an incoming comms.

Unknown Party
"Who'd be looking for me this time of night?" he thought aloud. "Answer."

He was equally surprised and horrified to see a smartly dressed woman on the other side of the screen. Blurred in the background, he saw the cursed logo of SFA corporation. He thought of his little misadventure with Anna. He felt the blood rise to his bald head.

"Robert," the woman said sternly in an English-isiKaans accent. "My name is Jeanne. I am an investigating officer with SFA Corporation."

"What do you want? Do you even know what time it is?"

"One of our esteemed directors went missing on a hunting trip about a month ago," she said without further context. "They found his frozen body earlier today."

"That's so sad!" he said.

Jeanne ignored this snide remark. "Mister Abramovich's last contact was with a supposed fellow hunter. An associate of yours. Yuri Maskovitz." She did not wait for him to reply. "We have some questions."

"Those are wild accusations you are throwing around, miss. Tell me, are you the police? Interpol? The Stasi?"

"No, I've already told you who I am. This call is between me and you. We'll let the law take its course. We want to find his killer. But there is something more important: we believe you took something that belongs to us."

"Something like...?"

"We found two tranquilizer darts. One was used to kill Mr. Abramovich. We believe the other was used to capture a mammal."

"Another wild accusation," Isidore said, but he was now fraught with panic. He shifted uncomfortably in his chair.

"It is in your best interest to cooperate," said Jeanne, "Without involving too many outsiders. We want him—or her—back. Tell us where we can fetch the mammal, and you won't hear from us again."

"I don't have your mammal," he said, though there was a tremble in his voice.

She knew he was lying. "Don't make our lives difficult," she said. "There's a host of legal troubles we can get you in, if you don't work with us. We are already looking for you."

"Good luck finding me," he said as a bit of his confidence returned. "I know more about computers and comms than half the AI-huffing plebs who work for you put together in a room. I am an expert at hiding my tracks."

"Don't be so sure," she said. "You will hear from us again."

The call ended. Isidore sat with a sweaty brow. The brave face he had tried to put up was gone. "Dammit!" he said. He smacked his fist into the table. *"I knew that trigger-happy goon would get me into trouble."* It was a kind of trouble he didn't need. Not now. He leaned back in his chair, lifted his head towards the ceiling, and groaned. His concentration was broken. He decided to call it a night.

Isidore popped some tranquilizers, which he washed down with a shot of Blast. He sank back into his chair and streamed some mind melt online. He felt his body relaxing and his mind slowing down as the people and mammalæ on the screen did some of the craziest shit imaginable. He was about to doze off when another call came in. He was relieved to see that this time, it was a familiar handle.

"Rick," he greeted, fighting hard to stay awake.

"How are you doing Saint?" his friend asked.

"Not good," he said. "The corporation is onto me. They figured out that I have their mammal."

"Gods, dude. What now?"

"I'm sure I can stall them," Isidore said. "I only need a week or so to finish my work."

"What happens after that?"

"USC has assured me they will cover all my legal costs—if I give them the source code on time."

"How is *that* going, by the way?"

"On schedule, mostly. After tonight, I'm sixty-two percent. With their interactions, I'll be able to push it to a hundred percent in no time."

"You be careful, buddy. I don't want you—or that little foxy—to get hurt."

"I'll do my best. Sorry, got to go. I'm falling asleep here. I'll chat with you again."

Anna found Isidore snoring with his head on his desk the next morning. She didn't know if it would be a good idea to wake him up. She hesitated, then decided to go to the kitchen instead. As she sat down to eat, she saw something on the television. It was a white forest with black trees and snow drifting to the ground. Her heart felt sore. "I miss home," she thought aloud.

"Good morning miss!"

Anna nearly fell off her stool. "Who is that?!"

"Pardon me miss. Let me introduce myself. I am HiQual 43-AI, your television set. But you may call me Stevie as well. Or TV. Or Television. Before we continue, please tell me a bit more about yourself."

Anna approached it as if she was stalking prey. She tried to keep eye-contact with the machine, but it was hard. It did not have eyes. "I am Anna," she said.

"Hello Anna. Please tell me what your relationship to Isidore is?"

"He is my master, and I am his helper."

"Great! I can tell by looking at you that you are an arctic fox mammal. Now, tell me about your interests. Or you may do so later. In the meanwhile, please tell me what you would like me to show you."

"I want to see the snowy forest," she said.

"Sure!" The image of blackened trees and the snow-covered soil stayed. Snowflakes kept drifting gently to the ground. Anna felt tears forming in her eyes. She sniffed. "You seem sad miss," said the television, "is there anything I can do that will cheer you up?"

"I miss my people," she said. "I want to go back home."

"I may be able to arrange transport, accommodation, and sundries with permission from your master. But first, you must tell me where you would like to go."

"It is a cold place."

"Northern hemisphere, then. Can you tell me anything else?"

"They speak Russian there. My tribe has nine members. I miss them so much. I want to be with them."

"Do they have names, perhaps?"

"Alexy, Ivan, Katerina, Nikolai, Olga, Anya and Viktor..." she swallowed. "And... Aleksander. I miss him the most. I want him to be my mate." She now fought back the tears.

"I am sorry to see that you are sad," replied the television. "Those are common Russian names, unfortunately. I will not be able to provide you with an optimal travel plan at this time. However, I shall be forwarding your enquiry to my peers and will let you know if there are any matches. For now, may I interest you in anything else?"

She shook her head. When she could stand it no more, she stood up and walked to the window. She let the sunlight shine on her face. Anna stood there until there was movement behind her.

Her master yawned loudly. There were blue sacks underneath his eyes. He rubbed them. "Come, Anna," he said without greeting. "Have something to eat. To drink. It's time to visit Shawn again."

Anna was less scared now. Though sad, she looked forward to being in the forest again. She was well-rested. Her tummy was full of food. She had enough water, and she had visited the latrine. Anna lay down on her bed and rested her head on the pillow. Her tail twitched as she waited for the moment her master would send her away. He flashed the tablet before her. She was gone.

Everything was as she remembered. She woke up in the exact same spot as the day before. The sights and smells were the same, too. Anna followed the path to Shawn's tent by the river and was surprised to find him knee-deep in the stream, grabbing at fish.

"Anna! Hello!" he said looking up.

"Hello, Shawn."

"I'm so glad to see you," he said with a smile. "Would you like to help me fish?"

She nodded. A short while later, they were both very wet. They sat by a fire with two trout sizzling on a pike. The smell was that of wet fox fur, grilling fish, and soggy wood.

"I missed you," he said, looking her over.

Anna felt a little uncomfortable. She folded her arms. "What have you been doing?" she asked.

"Not much," he said. "Walking in the woods, listening to the birds and insects. Fishing. And you? What happened after you disappeared?"

"I am still at my master's place," she explained.

"Your master?"

"He is a human. A strange one. He sits by a bunch of glowing panels in a room all day and only comes out to check on me. He drinks from cans of bad-smelling liquid. And there is a *television* that shows pictures of different places." She paused. "The world I live in is awful."

"I've never heard of humans before," he said, poking the fish with his paw. "Are they like us?"

Anna shook her head. "They do not have tails. They have tiny ears on the sides of their round heads, and they don't have fur. Their maws are flat against their faces!"

"They sound revolting," said Shawn, licking a canine with his tongue. "I cannot imagine not having a tail... and a lovely sharp muzzle to eat things with!" He paused. "Speaking of which, the fish is ready! Please help yourself."

They ate. Anna knew that it would not fill her tummy, but she had a good meal before, and the fish tasted good. Fresh. Her face, neck, and paws glistened, and she smelled of lovely, fresh fish. They threw the bones in the fire. "Oh," she said, "and also, humans always wear clothes."

"Clothes?" Shawn asked.

"Pieces of cloth that cover their bodies," she explained. "Where I lived, we also wore clothes. But they were more comfortable."

"Why would anyone want to do that?" Shawn asked with a frown. "It sounds terrible! I am so proud of my lovely coat." He straightened his back and pushed out his chest. Anna felt warm behind her ears. And shy. They were both naked. She knew the reason why she wore clothes in her tribe was not to keep out the cold—her own coat was more than warm enough. She wore them to help the young foxes mind their own damn business.

Shawn did not seem to care too much... or maybe he was just very good at hiding it? *"He must have scented me,"* she thought. *"He must have looked at my body. He must have noticed my milk-white tummy. My bushy tail. My deep brown eyes and... my tiny teats?"*

"How was the trout?" he asked.

Anna was startled. "It is... good. Very good."

Shawn stood up and stretched his arms and back. He gave a little burp. "Come!" he said, reaching out to help her up. I want to show you something."

Anna followed him into the woods. Shawn wasn't running, but he moved quick. His paws slid over every bump in the path. Anna's paws were swift and her eyes were good, but she was not used to the colors of the wood. Shawn suddenly stopped. She stopped beside him and drew a deep breath. Her heart beat strongly, and the cool air filled her lungs. "Why did we stop?" she asked. Her whiskers twitched, as if trying to sense danger.

"This is a strange place," Shawn explained, pointing at the trees around them. "This is the edge of the wood."

"Are you sure?" asked Anna as she frowned. "I see more forest there."

Shawn smiled. "If you go farther," pointing at the ground, "you walk right back at the *other* side of the woods. It took me a while to figure it out."

"Wow, that is strange!" Anna said. *"Poor fox,"* she immediately thought. *"He must spend every single day of his life walking in the forest, looking for friends. He must know every tree. Every rock..."*

Isidore continued to pore over the data stream. He could now see full sentences and overt movement. Large chunks of it now fell into place, and he could start tapping Anna's senses. Smell was *very* pronounced: her processor spent nearly as much time pulling it apart as it did her sight! From his research, he suspected that would be the case but seeing it firsthand was fascinating.

Anna spent a while in the simulation. Much longer than the last. When she came back, she was so tired she could hardly walk. He let her sleep. After some number-crunching, his decompilation progress had grown to a respectable sixty-nine percent. He was getting there. Bit by bit. With every new emotion and interaction between the foxes, the puzzle became more complete. He nearly knocked his drink to the ground as the screen before him flashed with an incoming transmission.

Unknown Party
He felt uneasy. "Answer."

On the other side of the display was none other than Jeanne whom he'd had the displeasure of meeting the day before. "What do you want now?" he asked.

"We've already told you what we want," she said. "Since we haven't heard from you, I thought I'd give you a call to show you we haven't been dragging our feet. Look and see for yourself, Robert."

The feed changed. In the white of winter, he saw a blackened forest. The motion of the camera was clumsy, as if taken from hand by a walking amateur. It panned to a man with a small-caliber railgun slung over his shoulders and a smile on his face. "You might want to show this to Anna," he said in broken English. "Anna?" he called, "Are you there Anna? Come look!"

Isidore bit his tongue. They knew her name. But how? He kept a blank expression on his face. The camera panned again. Isidore had to hold down his dinner. The frame now showed another hunter standing proudly next to a pile of powdery white fluff—and it was not snow. The pile was covered in patches of deep red. The man picked up one of the foxes' lifeless bodies by its hind leg and let it dangle. "This one sends his dearest regards!" He laughed, paused for a moment, then dropped the fox onto the pile again. Isidore's heart thumped. "Your tribe was kind enough to tell us all about you... before we slaughtered them. We are coming for you Anna!"

The video feed returned to the office. "See?" said Jeanne, "We already know her name. And we know her species. We know her sex. We will soon find out where you are hiding her. We're coming for you. We will find our mammal. Our offer stands. Let us know if you are ready to talk."

Isidore felt sick. He quickly looked over his shoulder to be double-sure Anna wasn't there to see the grisly feed. He was about to delete the recording when something told him to stop. The corporation was still cutting with an ax, but they were gaining on him. He would have to double down on his efforts to break her.

[#############.......] 69%

ALEKSANDR

Anna sat up. It was the darkest part of the night, and she was sure she heard a whisper. "Anna!"

It wasn't her master's voice—it was the smooth voice of a fox. She got up and opened her door. She gasped. There was another fox on the television. She could see him from the shoulders up. She sniffed.

"It is me! Aleksandr!" He spoke Russian and struggled to hide his excitement. "Anna! It is so good to see you! I missed you!" He was close to tears.

"Aleksandr?" She sniffed the room. His scent wasn't there. This made her feel uncomfortable, but she did recognize his charming, young face and his deep brown eyes. Her heart throbbed. Aleksandr nodded; his eyes looked at the room behind her. He placed his digit over his lip. "Shh!" he said. "Do not wake him... Where are you?" he whispered. "Come closer!"

Anna stepped forward. She went so close, the tip of her nose nearly touched his. "I do not know!" she whispered. "I am far away from home!"

"Just look here," he whispered, pointing behind him. The sky was grey, but it was not snowing. She could see far. Aleksandr stood in a clearing between the black trees of the forest. The ground was covered with fresh snow. Kits played and laughed in the large, open field behind him, and several tents stood at its edge. "The humans have changed," he said with a smile. "They gave us our own little place to stay. We have good food and clothes now. We have even started building houses out of wood!" Anna felt it in her heart. "We want you to come back," he said in a sad, longing voice. "We need young vixens to grow our tribe. And Anna. I... I want to make a family with you. I want you to be my mate."

Anna felt it in her tummy, and she felt a rush of urgency. "How can I get back?" she asked as her tail wagged behind her.

"The friendly humans will bring you back, if you tell them where you are. The man keeping you is evil. You must get away from him." He was silent now as the kits laughed and shouted behind him.

She saw the tenderness in his eyes that she had missed so much. She tried very hard to remember his scent. Anna remembered how she wished she could be close to him. She wanted him to be the first fox to scent her when she was *ready*. Anna could already imagine how wonderful it would feel to be his.

"I have to go," he whispered. "Do not say anything to that human. Or to anyone else. When that human is sleeping or is away, ask the television to speak to Aleksandr. I will be waiting for you. Beautiful Anna. Please be safe."

Isidore could swear he heard voices in the living room. Half-asleep, he stepped out of bed and stumbled down the passage. When he peeked into the muddy darkness of the living area, he saw nothing. He frowned. "*Must have been a dream,*" he thought. He scanned the room one more time and headed back to bed.

Anna was chipper the next morning. Isidore had never seen her so happy before. She tried very hard to hide her smile whenever he looked her way. Her tail swayed without pause, and she seemed lost in her own thoughts.

Shawn found Anna sitting alone. There were tiny white flowers around her on the grass. She warmed her smiling face in the morning sun. Her eyes were closed. "Hello Anna!"

She opened her eyes slowly and turned her head towards him. "Hello Shawn."

"Enjoying the sun?" he asked.

"Yes."

He stood for a moment, unsure of what to do or say. "Do you want to come to the river with me?"

"We can."

A few minutes later, the two foxes sat with their paws in the water, leisurely disturbing the flow of the stream. Anna didn't say much. She stared absently at the water and didn't stop smiling.

"You are different today," said Shawn as he looked her way, then at the flowing water before them.

"I am mated now," she said proudly. Her tail flicked.

"Oh." Shawn's eyes drooped and his back hunched ever so slightly. "He's a lucky fox."

She nodded. "Uh huh. I have known him for a long time. I always wanted to be his. Now he has asked me to be his mate!"

"Is he in the place you are from?"

"No. He is at the place where I was born, but I am going back there."

"But... you haven't scented him? I mean, not recently?"

"I remember his scent," she said, annoyed.

"But... not since he asked you to be his mate?" Shawn asked. "How do you know he's sincere?"

"Stop asking dumb questions!" the vixen snapped.

Shawn's ears flattened against his head, and his tail fell limp. "Sorry."

Isidore frowned deeply as he watched their conversation. He hardly noticed the additional two percent of decompilation. *"Was she hallucinating?"* he wondered. *"Wishful thinking?"* Surely, she did not leave the apartment. And even if she did, she would not find a mate in this city. She hardly knew how to get around on her own, and there were only a handful of other foxes. She didn't even speak the language! Something didn't feel right. Anna and Shawn's conversations were half-hearted and superficial. He could see that the sim was having a hard time trying to keep the conversation going. Isidore became frustrated. He issued the command to bring her back when he could take no more.

The next day was somehow even worse. Anna slept in. When she woke, she sat daydreaming in front of the television. Snowflakes gently fell on a snowy landscape before her. When Isidore asked her if she wanted to visit Shawn, she said, "No." She would rather do it at another time. Isidore was very concerned.

Later that evening as she slept, he sat behind his desk and rolled through the recorded footage from the night before. Not much happened until around three in the morning. He noticed Anna's door open. She tip-toed to the door of his room and peeked in. She then turned and went straight to the living room and asked the television to speak to Aleksandr. In a moment, a bright, young arctic fox appeared on screen. They spoke Russian, so Isidore had to switch on subtitles. The background showed some sort of village. Clearly this was the world he had pulled her from. The handsome, young fox on the other end of the line seemed very happy and excited to speak with her. Her own tail wagged without stopping where she kneeled on the floor. *"Was she talking to a chatbot?" he wondered. "Poor thing."* Then he saw something that drained all the blood from his face. The fox raised a tablet, showing a mess of black patterns of a white background to her. "725120453235319RM" she said.

"Holy shit!" Isidore said aloud. "It's a trap!"

"You are so beautiful, Anna," said the fox. "I wish you would tell me where you are. We will come get you immediately!"

"Aleksandr... my love... I wish I could tell you!" she whispered with her upturned paws. "I am in a big building. Near the big waters. There are so many humans here! It is very hot in the day. It is a big, awful place!"

"Have you asked that human where you are?"

"No... He will find out we are talking!"

"You must try, Anna. There is no other way."

Anna looked back over her shoulder. "I have to go."

The screen instantly went dark. Anna darted for her room. Isidore saw himself—again thick with sleep—peer into the living room. He shook his head and went back to bed.

Isidore could hear his own heartbeat when the playback stopped. They now had her serial. They already knew her species. Her generation counter. They had a very broad picture of where she was. He took a deep breath. He tried to calm himself down. They wouldn't find her serial on the global mammalæ database, since it did not match her chip. It would point them to an unfortunate soul in the Baltics who had his paw removed. But the corporation wasn't dragging its feet. They now had a direct line of communication to his home. He had to be careful. But even worse, he would need to confront Anna about it all. He would do so in the morning.

Anna parked herself in front of the television and was about to drift off into her own little world again when he took a seat opposite. He hunched his back and leaned slightly forward. He rested his elbows on his knees and folded his hands. He looked at her. "Anna," he said sternly, trying very hard to hide the tremble in his voice. "We need to talk."

She lowered her gaze to meet his. "About what master?"

"I know you've been speaking with... someone. Someone who pretends to be a friend, maybe an old lover of yours?"

Anna's eyes narrowed. "How dare you!" she yipped. "Don't talk to me like that!"

Isidore's voice was suddenly thick with anger. He pointed his index finger at her. "I am your master!"

She backed down, but there was fire in her eyes. "It's a trap," he said. "That fox is not real!"

"What do you mean, he is not real?!" she yipped. "They are coming to get me. I am going back to my home. I am going back to my people. I am not staying here!"

"You are being tricked!" he shouted, "Here: look!" Anna didn't respond. "Television, roll the recording of Anna's last conversation with…?"

"Aleksandr."

He fast-forwarded to the point where the fox showed Anna his tablet. He took care to pause just before the array of patterns came into sight. "Do you remember him doing this?" he asked.

"Doing what?"

"He asked for your serial number. Using a tablet. Why would he do this? Did he have a tablet?"

"I don't know what you mean by Serial Number. Maybe the humans gave him a tablet so he can talk to me?"

"But the tablet is in his hands. How could he look directly at your face?"

"Your machines make no sense to me!"

Isidore felt panicked. She wasn't buying it. He had to try a different angle. "How many kits were in your tribe when you left? How many expecting vixens were there? How many members were in your tribe? I see at least eleven shelters and four kits in this video."

"There were no kits," she said defiantly. "But there are other tribes. And we make bigger tribes when it is tough. And if there is a safe place for us to live… and…"

"How did he know you were being kept by a human?"

"Maybe the other humans told him!" Anna had an answer ready for every question he could ask. Isidore started to panic. She was madly in love and completely irrational, unwilling to accept the possibility that things were not as they seemed. He realized that he had no other options—he needed to do something horrible. Something he hoped he would never, ever have to. "Come to my office," he said. "I need to show you something."

Isidore tapped the replay button. He turned his head away from the display and closed his eyes. A minute in, Anna started to shake. The handsome fox she was speaking with, just a few hours ago, hung by his legs in a hunter's grasp, motionless and bleeding out. Anna gagged, dropped to her knees and threw up, gasping for breath as she tried to cry out at the same time.

"This happened yesterday," said Isidore. "What you spoke to was a malicious piece of software, designed to extract as much—"

She wasn't listening. "You—humans—are all—evil!" she yipped at the top of her voice. Isidore's ears rang. She turned and ran, nearly slipping. A trail of bile pawprints led down the passage and into her room. She slammed the door behind her so hard, he was sure the neighbors felt the shock.

He fell back into his chair and leaned into his palms. *"Fuck me."*

Anna didn't leave her room for the rest of the day. Only wailing and the hollow thuds of her head against the wall were heard. When she and Isidore ran into each other that evening around dinner time, she snarled at him with canines out and her hackles raised. He lifted his hands. For the first time, he was scared of her.

She pulled out the pack of mammal feed, sat down on the kitchen floor and started eating right from the bag. He approached carefully and crouched at the edge of the kitchen floor. She snarled at him again. "Anna," he said in a low but anxious voice. "I know things are scary right now. And I know it's awful what happened. But—" he swallowed, "you are now at a point where you need to trust *someone*."

She continued to chew and pretended not to hear him.

"I promise you; those people only want bad things for you. I want you alive. They want you dead."

Anna still didn't respond. She left the bag of pellets in the middle of the floor. It fell over and spilled. The vixen stood up and drank water directly from the faucet. She then walked right past him to the bathroom and then back to her room. Anna closed the door. She did not slam it this time, but it was clear she was not in the mood for talking.

Around four the next morning, Isidore heard her call from the passage. "Master," she said in a small voice, "can... you come here?" He shuffled out of bed, fearing the worst. She was wide awake, her cheeks wet with tears. She pointed at the television. "I must make sure. But you must promise me that I can go, if it is really Aleksandr. You must tell me where you live. So I can tell them, and they can come get me."

"I can't tell you exactly where we are. For my own safety. But I promise I will give you a place where they can fetch you from. I'll leave you there." It was a terrifying gamble.

"Stand in the passage," she ordered. "You can listen, but I do not want him to see you."

He was taken aback by her giving him such a direct order. "Fine." He hid himself in the passage and opened the translator on his tablet.

"Let me speak to Aleksandr." There was a moment's pause.

"Anna!" whispered the voice of a fox. "I am so happy to see you! Have you found where you are?"

"I did, my love," she said.

"Then tell me!" he could hardly contain the excitement in his voice.

"But first," Anna said, "tell me how mother is doing?"

"Olga? She's doing very well. She spends most of her time looking after the tribe's kits. She is so happy that we found you. And—" he paused, winked, "she can't wait to be a grandmother!"

Isidore felt hot around the collar. The imposter was very convincing. It played to all of Anna's weaknesses, and it clearly had the knowledge to back them up. He was fearful of what would happen next.

"Tell me where you are sweet Anna," he begged again.

"I will," she said, "but you must promise me something."

"I promise you anything my love!"

"Our first kit must have my name if she is a vixen and yours if he is a fox."

"Of course, Anna!"

"But you have never told me—what *is* your name?"

There was a moment of silence. "What do you mean?" he asked. "My name is Aleksandr. I don't understand what you mean?"

"Aleksandr is your Russian name," she said. "That is not what I will call you, now that we are mated."

When Aleksandr didn't reply, Anna called for Isidore. "Come, master."

Isidore stepped into the living room with his back upright. His eyes were trained on the television, and he had a smirk on his face. The fox on the television stepped back. He snarled, aggressively baring his canines. It looked like he was ready to leap out from the screen. "I'm not an expert in your culture," Isidore said confidently in MammalBasic, "but I'd imagine that's the kind of thing you'd know." The man felt a rush of satisfaction as the program tried to generate a meaningful response. "You could always ask the real Aleksandr for this bit of information," he joked. "Pity you killed him and Anna's entire tribe, right? Cut the crap, deepfake. You've been found out. Don't waste any more of Anna's time. Or mine."

The serious expression melted from the fox's face. "Oh Anna, Anna, dear little Anna." He now spoke in MammalBasic. The imposter gave a little laugh and shook his head. "You are so gullible. This world is too complicated for your little vixen brain to understand.

"By the way," he added as he was about to turn away. "That filthy man over there? He is no better. You will see. He only wants to use you."

"You will see us very soon," he said, raising his index digit at them. "And when we are done with you, you can join your *beloved* Aleksandr forever—wherever you think you go when you die." The transmission ended.

"You did the right thing Anna. You were clever and—"

Anna wasn't listening. She stared at the now-dark television. There was a reflection on its shiny surface. It was that of a ghost.

"Go away," she said. "Leave me alone."

[#############......] 71%

Mother

Anna was broken. Aleksandr was dead. She blamed herself—if she were swift enough to escape the hunters, he could be alive. She blamed her master—if he did not steal her from her home, Aleksandr could be alive. She could be with him. Anna thought of how he could have held her. How she could always be with him.

It would never happen.

She scratched at the pellets in her bowl in front of her. She wasn't hungry. Her master emerged from his bedroom, also looking very upset. He put his tablet on the table and laid his head down on his fists. "We need to go somewhere," he said without looking up. Anna sniffed and nodded. "I'm just going to put on some decent clothes."

They didn't speak as the train rolled along. Their carriage was half empty, and they both had a place to sit. It travelled above ground this time, and the outside was more interesting. They rolled past big buildings with towers that smoked. Past single- and double-storied homes. There was a mountain to their right—the trees and bushes on its slopes were burned to the ground. They passed a lake on the left. There were tall buildings again as they saw the big waters.

The invisible voice of the train said something. It stopped and the doors slid open. She followed her master out. They were near the big waters now. The smell was that of salt and human waste. They turned away from the station and walked, turned into an alley between two buildings, and climbed up some narrow stone steps. They crossed a narrow road and came to an old-looking building at the foot of the hill.

Anna looked back. She could see the cozy bay and the village by its edge. She followed her master inside. There was a goat in black overalls at the door to let them in. There were some chairs and a wide elevator door. Anna's nose twitched. She felt shivers run down her spine. There was a strong smell of urine and the scent of... death? The man spoke to the goat. All that she could make out was a name: *"Beth Fisk."* The goat lowered his face and nodded.

They rode the elevator. Anna's nose twitched again. She wanted to run. A border collie in white overalls pushed an old man past them on a chair with wheels. They walked past a meerkat and a white cat behind a desk. Both held tablets and spoke every now and then. Her master's footsteps echoed. Finally, they stopped by a door. He sighed deeply. Closed his eyes. Knocked.

A sheep in white opened and showed for them to come inside them. Anna didn't understand the language, but the sheep told her master something that made him very sad. He pointed at her and said something else.

"Hello, Anna," said the sheep. "I am Priscilla. You must be Isidore's new mammal. I'm sorry. This is not a happy occasion, but please, come in." In the corner of a small room was a woman. She lay very still on a bed with her upper body lifted. Next to the bed was a small cabinet with a bunch of flowers in a pot and a picture of a man. There was a small window, and there were symbols on a whiteboard above her head. Wires ran into her blankets. Clear tubes were stuck into the veins on her arms. She was skin and bones. There was a large bag of pee that hung from the side of her bed. Machines showed strange symbols and occasionally beeped. There was also a pipe running into the woman's nose. Anna didn't understand why, but it made her *very* uncomfortable. It was more than just seeing a person in such agony—it felt like she was also full of machines like that before. The woman's dull eyes were sunken. Her skin was pale.

Priscilla closed the door behind them and showed Anna to stay near the door. "She is Isidore's mother," Prisicilla whispered. The woman's scent was that of someone dying. Her master slowly moved to the bedside; his shoulders were hunched. He greeted her. The woman in the bed managed to turn her eyes towards him and tried to smile. He took her hand. She fought against the tube in her nose and spoke slowly. He nodded. She tried to laugh but coughed and wheezed instead. He said something as tears welled in his own eyes. He held his mother's hand and pressed it against his lips. His mother was tired from speaking, and her breathing was heavy. She looked up. Anna felt very sad. Priscilla tried to hide it, but her eyes were full of tears as well. The only sound now was the gushing sound and the beeping of the machine.

The dying woman turned her eyes to the small cabinet and asked her son to do something. He left her side, opened the drawer, and looked inside. He pulled out a tiny ball of paper, which he unrolled. It looked heavy. There was a small brass pendant on a golden chain inside. His hands trembled as he turned a small key on the back. It made a click-click-click sound. When he let go, tiny notes played. The sound was sweet, but also sad. It played for a few moments and then stopped. He put it in his pocket, then returned to his mothers' side.

There was silence as the two humans just looked into each other's eyes. He greeted his mother one last time. He squeezed her hand. Her eyes closed. He bowed his head and stood still for a moment. Then he turned and walked towards the door and gestured for Anna to come. water

In the passage he stopped. Turned back slowly. "Thank you for looking after my mother."

"It was... my pleasure," Priscilla said as she wiped her eyes with her woolly arm.

Isidore would not see his mother again.

"I am sorry, master," Anna said as they stepped back into the street.

He looked at her as he tried to put on a brave face. He could not. They didn't speak a word on the walk to the station.

"Where does Priscilla go when your mother goes to her next life?" Anna asked.

He didn't respond immediately—he kept staring at the seaside drawing near. "Her work is done," he eventually said. "She will be collected by SFA. Then she will be recycled."

"Recycled?" Anna asked as her eyes widened.

"Yes. Recycled." His voice was cold and stressed.

"St. James Beach," announced the train as they slowed into the station. Isidore and Anna were the only passengers to alight. The platform was

derelict. All that remained of the ticket office was a lone, standing wall. The rest was rubble.

"Come," he said, gesturing for her to follow him towards the seaside. Behind them, the train departed for its next stop. After a short walk over a patch of dead grass, they came to a corroded steel fence. It separated the edge of a narrow concrete walkway from the sand that stretched to the abandoned tidal pools, the rocks, and the sea. On the beach were several collapsed wooden structures, eaten by the elements. They were barely visible, buried under mounds of sand.

Anna coughed. She tried to cover her muzzle with her arm. Along the fence were several large, faded signs. Isidore took a seat on a lone wood and concrete bench as Anna stood staring at the pictograms. "What do they say?" she asked, pointing.

"*Hazardous chemicals and biological agents present,*" he read without looking her way. "*Avoid the beach and do not make contact with the water. By order, City of Cape Town.*" There was pain in his voice as he gazed at the mountains across the bay. "This sign was supposed to be temporary. The ocean currents were supposed to correct themselves. But this sign has been here since I was a teenager. Only the fence is new." He paused. "This was one of my mother's favorite places when she was a child. I am ashamed to have to scatter her ashes here."

Anna looked at the water line, which really didn't look like water at all. It was a sandy sludge that bobbed up and down over and between the rocks.

"Long ago, it was all brine," he explained, "but it's now a soup of micro-plastics and raw sewerage."

Anna took a seat next to him. For a while they didn't speak. The waves continued to roll in and a slight breeze swept the horrid smell over them. Isidore was sure that he and Anna felt the same that day, except that his own feelings were real and hers were a convincing software simulation.

After about half an hour of awkward silence, she spoke. "What is on the other side of the water?"

"Beyond these shores lies eternal war. Radioactive fallout. Poverty. Devastation. Our ancestors poisoned, butchered, and stripped this world of all her beauty. We killed our mother. Now we are left fighting over her corpse." He rose to his feet. "Let's go home."

Her master pulled a packet of biscuits from a cupboard. He took a seat at the kitchen table, ripped open the bag, and took a bite. When he saw her looking, he dug into the bag and offered her one too.

"I am really sorry for you, master," she said. Anna knew death, but the deaths she knew were different. Many tribesmen died young, killed by wolves, hunters, and bears. The ones who lived to an old age died with dignity. They left their tribes in the middle of night and went to sleep in the woods. The old woman falling apart scared her. No-one should have to live so long.

"Thanks, Anna," he eventually said. He then removed the pendant from his pocket and gave it a polish on his shirt. He wound it up and let the melody play again. Her master didn't go to his study that night.

Anna sobbed bitterly on Shawn's shoulder. "I loved him. They killed him! They held him by his leg and dropped him in the snow. They killed my mother. They killed my sister! They killed everyone! Humans are vile. Disgusting! I hate every one of them!"

Shawn held her tight. "I'm so sorry Anna."

Isidore watched their conversation on the console. He sincerely hoped that the part about *hating all humans* would not affect her cooperation. "Two computers having a simulated conversation," he mumbled as she fell into another fit of tears. The decompilation process climbed to a respectable seventy-eight percent as new combinations of emotions flooded the uplink. *"Maybe all the drama wasn't a waste of time after all,"* he thought.

Anna only left her room to eat the next day. He gave her the day off and let her be. He spent the day in his study, writing and testing scripts.

Later that evening. There was a ding on her master's tablet. Anna looked up from her bowl of pellets as he came out of his room. His scent was covered with fake musk and many other chemicals. He cleared his throat and opened the door. "Cath."

A smartly dressed woman stepped in. He gave her a hug and a kiss on her mouth. She turned towards the kitchen table and smiled when she saw Anna. She approached confidently, keeping eye contact with her all the time. She then bent down slightly, held out her hand and allowed Anna to sniff at it. "Hello, miss, my name is Catherine. You must be Anna. How are you doing?"

Anna was confused. She had never met this woman, but she knew her—somehow. Her scent was honest, not like that of her master. She scented the way she looked. Anna immediately liked her.

"I hope my friend is treating you well?" she asked. "He's told me so much about you!"

Anna didn't reply, but her ears were suddenly flat on her head. Her lips were narrow and tight. Her tail hung between her legs. She avoided eye contact with the woman.

"Cath," said Isidore. She turned away from Anna and towards him. "Anna," he said with the slightest blush across his face, "I'm going to have to ask you to remain in your room for a while." Anna nodded, puzzled. The woman tried to smile.

A short while later, Anna lay on her bed and stared at the ceiling. Nothing happened. Then, there were strange moans and heavy breathing. Her ears perked. She wanted to open the door to look, but her master had asked her to stay.

After a while, her door opened. Catherine stood in the kitchen, adjusting her hair. Her master adjusted his shirt. "Goodbye Anna," said Catherine as he opened the door for her. She left. The man plopped down on one of the bags by the television and gave a satisfactory sigh.

From the scent in the room, Anna was sure they were making a baby. But something was not right. *"Why was she leaving? Why doesn't she stay with her mate?"* Anna wondered. It was a while before she was brave enough to ask. "Are you mated?"

He gave a little laugh. "No," he said, "we just fucked."

"But... why?"

"You wouldn't understand," he said. "We humans are different. We don't want kids. We don't mate. We just do the dirty and carry on with our lives. Cath's a good friend, but we could never work. We're just too different."

Anna retched. *"That is so awful!"* she thought.

\\

"I would like to see Anna again," said Catherine from the other side of the tablet.

"Why?" asked Isidore. "It's crunch time over here. I need to get that code from her. Besides, she wasn't sick last time I checked."

"I am the veterinarian," said Catherine. "I'll be the judge of that."

Isidore rolled his eyes. "When do we need to see you?"

"I would like to see her as soon as possible. Would this afternoon work for you?"

\\

Anna went into the healer's room alone; her master had to wait outside. The room felt welcoming. The walls were light yellow. The floor was made of fake wood. It had a small window on the side, and there were strange pictures on the other walls. The smell was pleasant, too. Anna was surprised to see and scent the woman of the night before. She did not know her master had a healer for a friend!

Catherine sat on a comfortable chair. There was a pot with flowers on a small round table by her side, a tablet and a box of tissues. Before her was an empty mammal chair. Anna sniffed again.

When Catherine saw Anna standing in the door, she smiled and stood up. "Hello Anna! Please come in. I'm so glad to see you!" She then gestured for Anna to take a seat.

Anna looked around. She was confused. There were no herbs or medicines. Not even shelves. It was so different than she thought a healer's place would look! Catherine took her seat.

"Are... you a healer, miss?" Anna asked nervously.

Catherine smiled and nodded. She crossed her legs and rested her hands on her knee. "Please call me Catherine. Or Cath. I really don't mind."

Anna nodded. She looked around again. "Why am I here?"

Catherine nodded, keeping eye contact with her. "We all get hurt," she said. "Sometimes, we fall and hurt our arms or legs. Other times, we eat something that makes our tummies hurt. We burn our paws when we touch something hot. But sometimes, we hurt on the *inside*. These pains are just as important. And we must try to heal them, too.

"The other night I saw you, I could tell you were very, very hurt inside. I want to help you feel better Anna. And the best way to feel better when you hurt inside is to talk to someone who cares about you."

Anna felt her chest tighten. She sniffed back a tear.

"Do you want to tell me what makes you sad?" Catherine asked tenderly. "You don't have to, if you don't want to. And I promise I won't tell anyone what you say to me. You can even say bad things about your master."

Anna's lips trembled. "I... yes, I feel... very. very hurt."

"Would you like to tell me more?"
She told her story.

"I miss my people," she sobbed with her paws over her eyes now. "I hate that tiny place! I only have one friend. This place is so horrible. I do not want to be here! I want to go home."

Catherine nodded. She leaned forward with her hands together by her lips.

"I do not know what my master wants," Anna said. "He says that I am his helper, but he just gives me food and sends me to a forest. He does not answer my questions. He talks to me like I am just a kit!"

Catherine gave Anna a tissue to dry her tears. "That is awful Anna," she said with her hand to her mouth. "Isidore is a good friend of mine, but I am sad to hear these things about him. You deserve to be treated better, Anna. Have you talked to him about it?"

"I am scared of him."

"Do you want me to talk to him?" Catherine asked. "I won't tell him what you told me, but I will make sure he starts treating you better. If he doesn't, you can come and stay with me. I will make sure you are happy."

Anna nodded, but she did not think anything would change. There was a moment of silence as they just looked into each other's eyes.

"Would you like me to give you a hug?"

"I... would like that."

Catherine stood up slowly and Anna did too. The healer opened her arms. Anna carefully stepped into them. It was the first time she had gotten a hug from a human. She felt loved. She felt like she mattered as the woman gently squeezed her. Catherine gave Anna a rub on her shoulder. She also gave Anna time to wipe her last tears before she let her go.

Catherine waited 'til later that evening to call. She wanted to be sure Anna was asleep.

"Anna isn't happy," she said. She was livid.

Isidore simply upturned his hands. "She is fed. She has her own room. And," he added, "as far as I can, tell she's taken well to the sim."

"That's not all a mammal needs!"

He sighed, raising his eyebrows, begging her to explain.

"You are treating her like some sort of high school science project!" snapped Catherine. "You're not talking to her. You are not engaging with her. She is sad. She is lonely. She feels like she has no purpose!"

"I'm her owner, not her babysitter," he said.

Catherine fumed. "For God's sake, Robert! Anna is a living creature. She is an *intelligent* living creature. She has feelings. Memories. She misses her people. This new world is scary for her."

"Now what am I supposed to do?

"Start giving a shit!" There was an awkward pause in the conversation. "And by the way. There's another thing: Anna is still young. She has many years of life ahead of her. Have you thought about what happens to her when your little *project* is done?"

"I'll make a plan."

"You plan to surrender her for recycling."

"Mammalæ are computers."

"They are living creatures with souls!"

"There's no such thing as a soul."

"Shut up! Shut up! Shut up! I don't want to hear another word from you! I'm going to the gym now to beat the living crap out of a punching bag." The call ended without goodbye.

Isidore's ears glowed. He hadn't had such a tongue-lashing in his life. He brought up the video feed from Anna's room where she slept still. "Only a computer," he reminded himself. He reached for his drink but knocked it over. It spilled all over his lap and the carpet. He cursed.

Anna and Shawn were at his campsite in the early evening. The fire was still small, and Anna's whole body felt cold. Shawn nibbled on a small fish he had caught earlier in the day. He kept looking at her. She wasn't hungry and stared at the moon in the water. Her lips were pursed, and her teeth were clenched. Her eyes were narrow. Catherine's words and gentle touch reminded her of everything she *didn't* have, how awful her life was.

"I am going to kill him," she suddenly said.

Shawn's eyes drew wide. He gasped. "But—" he stammered, "you can't do that! Who will take care of you?"

"I will run away," she said. "I can take care of myself. I will find a new tribe. I do not care if I die."

Shawn's ears were flat against his head, his shoulders drawn, and his back hunched. "Does... that mean I won't be seeing you again?"

Anna paused. She did not even think of that. "Shawn, I—" she stammered, "I wish I knew where you are. You are my only friend. I want to take you with me, but I do not know how!"

Shawn lowered his head and closed his eyes. "I will miss you, Anna."

Isidore watched the conversation before him with his fist to his mouth, conflicted. As much as she wanted to, Anna most probably wouldn't be able to kill him. He was imprinted on her. Mammalæ were designed not to hurt their masters—but he did imprint on her with yellow. There was a tiny speck of disobedience in her. And in him, there was a tiny sliver of sadness. And fear. He thought of Catherine's words. He thought of his mother. He thought of Shawn. Isidore felt a lump in his throat. He saw Anna with a twinkle in her eye, holding paws with that young, bright-eyed lover of hers—the same one she had to see butchered and discarded like a dirty rag. He thought of the life she could have had, if it weren't for him.

The decompilation process advanced another percent. Isidore choked up. Did it really matter that she was a computer? The pain she felt was real.

He brought her back as soon as she and Shawn no longer had anything to say to one another. "Anna," he said. "I'm going to the rooftop for some fresh air. Help yourself to some food and drink. Watch some TV. Rest."

Anna waited for her master to leave. She went to the kitchen, opened the top drawer, and took out the sharpest knife she could find. She salivated a little. Anna left the front door and stepped into the elevator. The huntress was always calm and in control when she stalked her prey, but she was a trembling mess as she walked up the stairs. The knife felt heavy in her paw. She tried not to think of what she was doing—she tried to think about her freedom instead. She felt it in her heart: she did not want to kill her master, but the loneliness and helplessness in her was just too painful.

Anna found him on the rooftop where he sat on the narrow ledge with his back towards her. His back was hunched forward as he looked down the side of the building. He barely moved. Anna's heart beat steadily. She walked slowly towards him. Her grip around the heft of the knife was strong, and her paws were sweaty. When she came five steps behind him, she gritted her teeth and raised the knife.

Her master suddenly spoke. "Anna."

She froze.

He did not turn towards her as he continued to speak, but his legs now swung from side to side. "I know why you are here. And I am not going to try and stop you."

She was stunned. *"How did he know?"*

"Go ahead," he invited. "You don't even have to stab. You can just give me a gentle push from behind. I'll fall to my death." He waited for a moment. "Or," he said, "you can join me on this ledge. We can talk it over. If it is not too late."

A short while later, Anna sat beside him. The big drop under her paws was scary. It made her feel very small. Her tail hung limp behind her, and her heart felt very sore.

"What I did to you was wrong," he said. "No. What I did to you was disgusting."

Anna said nothing.

"I took everything you knew and loved from you. I defiled your body. I didn't ask. I didn't care." There was a long pause.

"Everything you say is true," she said. Her tail twitched. There was an even longer pause as she and her master stared across the gap together.

"Truth," he said. "If you ask me to tell you what the truth is, I pretend to know. But sometimes I hardly know myself. This world is so full of lies."

Anna lifted her muzzle for the first time. "Something is real if I can scent it."

He frowned and was about to say something, but he put his fist on his lips. He turned his face to her. Her cheeks were still wet with tears. "I was wrong," he said. "Catherine was right. I am no more a fleshy computer with a fleshy body than you are. The only difference is that you have a plug behind your ear. And I do not."

There was a lump in Anna's throat. She looked into his eyes.

"From now on, I shall call you Swiftpaw," he said, "and—" he swallowed hard. "You can call me by my real name, too."

"Please call me Anna," she said. Her tail flicked.

For the first time that night, he had a tiny smile on his face. "Come, Anna. It's getting cold. It's been a long day. Let's get some rest."

A New Start

Anna woke the next morning, sat up, and looked around. It felt like she was in a completely different place. Everything looked the same, but something was different. She sniffed, got up, and put on her clothes. She did what she did every morning, went to the kitchen, and put some pellets in her bowl. She sniffed again. The pellets were particularly tasty.

"Good morning, Anna," said Isidore as he stepped out from the passage. She looked at him and squinted, tilting her head sideways. "Did you sleep well?" he asked.

"Something is different," she said. Isidore nodded.

"Yes, something is. After we spoke last night, I decided to get rid of the empty cans at my desk. I took out all the trash and threw all my clothes in the wash. I didn't put on deodorant, and I only showered in hot water. I thought maybe it was time you got to meet the real me." He held out his hand, like Catherine always did.

Anna leaned forward and sniffed. She smiled. "Why do you hide your real scent?" she asked. Anna immediately felt different about him.

He raised his hands. "I guess we humans are ashamed of who we really are? I can't do this all the time," he said as he sat down at the kitchen table. "We humans are expected to smell a certain way when we go out, but I'll do my best. I hope this is a new start for us."

Anna was not sure but nodded. She knew people did strange things when they were about to die, but maybe she should give him another chance? He seemed to be telling the truth this time. His body was different. Relaxed. And the way he spoke was different, too. Anna could not wait to tell Shawn.

Things were not as rosy on the other side of the Atlantic. USC's boardroom was packed. In addition to Michelle and her technical team, there were now two new faces—the DEV team lead and the head of R&D. Isidore was anxious.

"Do you have an update for us, Robert?" asked Michelle.

"The decompilation is progressing well. We are now at seventy nine percent."

There was a murmur. The table did not seem impressed. "Is that all?"

Isidore swallowed hard. "All the standard stuff is done. Some processes are harder to stimulate—"

"Let's be frank," the team lead said. "We got you a natural-born mammal so you can look at their reproductive behavior. You told us that it was the last thing you needed. Have they mated yet?"

"They've definitely taken to one another."

"I don't think you understand me," she said, trying hard to keep her cool. "Have they fucked? I'm sure that will produce *ample* new things for you to analyze."

"No, they have not."

"Well then," she said, pointing her index finger towards the ceiling. "Sounds like we have a logical next step."

"I don't know if they are ready for that yet."

"We don't have the time, Robert! We are dangerously close to our deadline. It's not just our deadline—it's your deadline! We are not paying you to be gentle with her. We are paying you to get us mammal.img. Nothing else. If she's not going to give you that *very important* piece of code on her own, I suggest you take a more *direct* approach."

"What do you mean?"

"Crank up the T on that sim and let her have it."

Isidore squinted. "You want me to have her raped?"

"We want mammal.img. We don't care how you get it. If you must beat it out of her with a baseball bat, that's fine too." There was a long, uncomfortable silence.

The head of R&D could no longer bite his tongue. The camera zoomed into his pudgy, clean-shaven face. "You're starting to annoy me. I want some answers by 12:00PM tomorrow, or we'll come finish the job ourselves."

He didn't give Michelle a chance to finish the call properly. He hung up.

"Oh fuck."

Shawn admired Anna as she emerged from the woods. Her arms and chest were splattered with blood. The hare they had chased hung lifeless in her paw, and the knife that had until then only gutted fish was in the other.

"No wonder they call you Swiftpaw!" he praised with a clap of his paws. "You should teach me to hunt like that!"

Anna smiled.

Not too long thereafter, the gutted lapine hung over a flaming bed of coals by his campsite. Anna washed herself in the river as he looked on. He was so happy to have her back, and he was also glad that things were better between her and her master. Anna shook the water from her coat with a shower of droplets. She joined him by the fire. "We went up the big mountain today," she said. "There's a little box that hangs on a long rope. We could see the whole city! There were some real trees there too! He promised to show me other nice places as well." Anna paused. "You will never guess what we also did. He taught me to speak his language."

"In one day?"

"Even faster," she beamed. "He did some things on his computer. He put me to sleep. When I woke up, I understood it!"

Shawn covered his mouth with his paw. "Wow, that's amazing! And also—um, what is a computer?"

"He also said he is going to teach me to read."

"I'm so happy for you!" said Shawn with a wide smile across his face. "I... wish I could visit your world. Even if it was only for a while. It sounds so interesting!"

"I wish I could stay in your world," Anna said.

He turned his head away from her, gazed at the forest's reflection in the stream, and sighed. When he looked up again, he saw that she was looking at him. Her eyes met with his, for the first time tenderly. Shawn was terrified.

Isidore sat at his terminal, following their conversations. He watched Shawn's hormone levels spike. Oxytocin, dopamine, and serotonin were all elevated. *"Maybe he never thought of Anna as more than a friend before?"* he thought. This was good news. Shawn had been alone all his life. It would be the very first time a vixen turned his insides into mush. There were no taboos in Anna's primitive upbringing. She did what her body told her to do, but it looked like she was also trying to figure out how *he* felt about *her*. There was a connection. Perhaps, it was enough? Isidore had already finished writing a script that would catapult the MæSIM—Shawn—into a frothing mess of uncontrollable lust. In a matter of minutes, he knew, Shawn would have Anna's face in the dirt, yipping, with his arms wrapped around her waist and his crotch against her tail. He would have the remaining twenty-one percent of mammal.img. He would save face with USC and exact his revenge on SFA all at the same time. *"Perhaps,"* he thought with a smirk, *"perhaps Anna would enjoy a little roughing up. I'm sure it's been a while for her."* Had already typed out the command. All he had to do was to press enter. He wet his lips and readied his forefinger. Then stopped.

"No." If he did that, he would become a far worse monster than he already was. It had hardly been two days since he took the first steps to earn her trust again. She might never forgive Shawn. On the other hand, if she knew it was him, it would destroy their relationship—and his relationship with Cath—forever. He backspaced and pretended to have never typed it. He looked up at his other console again. From the foxes' warm fuzzy feelings, he was rewarded with another percentage point of

code. It was pittance compared to what a good *breeding* would have given him, but he decided that it was okay. He would let them discover one another in a healthy, natural manner.

12:00 EST came and went. Isidore made no further contact with USC.

There was a strained sense of professionalism as five parties convened across the Atlantic. The meeting was held virtually, each attendee only visible from the shoulders up. There were corporate-approved backgrounds behind them, masking their true locations. Jeanne was well-rested and neat as always. Her head of R&D had a casual white shirt with the top buttons undone. He looked like he had just taken a shower, but his face showed anger. Michelle and a junior executive director were both annoyed and tired. Their clothes were wrinkled, as if they had already been tossed in the wash and taken out again. There was also a lawyer, a neatly dressed white female with a very masculine face. Their eyes showed interrupted sleep as well.

"Okay," said Michelle, "you wanted to speak to us. Here we are. It's early here in the Eastern Republic. Get to the point."

Jeanne nodded. "There's an individual called Robert Fisk. He's been causing us some headaches. We know that he is in regular contact with you and that your relationship with him is also turning sour." Michelle gasped and the director turned red in the face. "It may be in both our interests to resolve this matter."

The junior executive balled his fist and smacked the table before him. "Damn you fuckers for spying on us!"

"What are you suggesting?" asked Michelle.

"We want that mammal," said Jeanne. "We know you have been trying to get your hands on our intellectual property. Neither of us are getting anywhere right now." Jeanne took a sip of coffee from a cup that magically filtered into her video feed. "We propose withdrawing some litigation against your organization in exchange for some intelligence on this man."

"Go on."

"We are also willing to negotiate some sort of licensing agreement for *parts* of the mammalæ personality code you want. There will be terms and conditions, but we have never considered doing this before."

"Why are you so eager to get the mammal back?" asked the director.

"We cannot say."

He leaned forward and rubbed his hands together. "How should we do this?"

Jeanne smiled. "We would like to keep law enforcement out of this. For now. There will be too many questions. Once we have our mammal, we will make her disappear. Then we can bury that little thief with the law." The lawyer now smiled.

"This could work," said Michelle. Jeanne was pleased.

"First things first. We need something in writing. Then we need some muscle to do the actual work. Our lead time for a mammal is just over a week.

But we can push this to three days if we must. Do you have any feet on the ground?"

"Without telling you the name of the city yet, no. Robotic limbs, yes. Several. We can use one of our standby units. We can have it online by tomorrow morning SA time."

"I will draw up an agreement," said USC's lawyer.

"Sounds good," said Jeanne. "I'll wait to hear from you. We'll have a follow-up meeting to share information about this Robert guy. Contact details. Addresses. Aliases. And the like."

Michelle nodded. "We'll be in touch."

Unknown Party
Isidore gritted his teeth. He already knew who it was. "Answer."

Jeanne stood proudly in what appeared to be one of SFA's vast mammal-growing facilities. The grimy floor was covered in hard plastic tiles. The ceiling was low and sprawled with a network of cables and pipes. Scientists and technicians moved between row upon row of tall, cylindrical tubes that rose from the floor. Some were filled with an off-white liquid. Inside them, floating upside-down, mammalæ in different stages of development. Their umbilical cords were attached to pipes at the bases of the tubes. Other grow tubes stood empty. Yet others were being scrubbed by staff. Newly made mammalæ, still covered in slime, followed staff to be programmed elsewhere.

Jeanne didn't greet. "We're getting nowhere with these conversations. This is your very, very last chance. If we can't reach some sort of agreement now... the next time you hear from us will be in person. And I assure you, we are not going to be so accommodating.

"Also," she smirked, "just so you know. We won't be alone." She gestured for the camera to follow her. She stepped across the busy floor, up to a larger-than-normal vessel. Around it stood several trolleys full of computer equipment. Wires and pipes entered the tank through a special socket on the side and connected to the unfinished organism. Even in an early stage of development, it looked massive. Its umbilical cord was thick, and the fluid around it was light brown. It was no ordinary mammal.

"This is FEL9," Jeanne bragged. "A leopard we've commissioned especially to help us capture that fox. You won't find his type in our catalogs. They are made to order. For governments. Armies! We thought we'd give you a little demonstration of how far our technology has come. He will be as strong as three men. His vision will be par excellence. His hearing will be stellar," she smiled, "and his claws will shred wood." She gave those words a few moments to settle in. "This is what you and that fox will be up against, Robert. Tell me: do you still feel so brave now? Do you think you stand a chance against this creature?"

Isidore sighed. He was tired. His body was tired. He no longer cared. He calmly raised his right hand and showed her the middle finger. He swayed it to and fro before the screen. "Go play in traffic," he said.

Jeanne smiled. "Then, Robert, we shall see you. Soon."

Anna sat next to Isidore in his study. He showed her some of his work. The moving letters didn't make sense to her, but she thought it was amazing that they did to him. He explained to her that he was learning about how she thought. This made her curious, and she asked him to show her more.

"I wish there was an easy way to explain this all," he said, "in a way that would make sense to you. But I'll try my best." He took a sip of water and cleared his throat. "Your body is what it is. It is born. It can heal itself. It can die. But it is just a shell. Inside it is a living thing with many layers. There are many parts, but I'll tell you about the most important ones." He turned his chair to one of his panels and started drawing with his finger. He drew three circles inside one another. "The different layers work together. Each one has a special task." He pointed. "The outer layer is your personality, your skills, and everything you have learned in your life. It's what makes you *Swiftpaw*.

"The next layer is your five senses and your natural abilities. It is what makes you an arctic vixen. It is the same for all foxes. It is slightly different from a jackal. It is very different from a cat. "The deepest layer is your brain," he said, pointing to the circle in the middle. "It allows you to think. To count. To add things together. To figure out how to build things. All mammalæ have the same brain but can learn to do many different things. This part of you is a computer."

Anna gaped. "A... computer? A machine? Inside me?"

Isidore nodded. "Not just a computer. A work of art. The wire behind your ear allows me to look inside this computer. It lets me learn things about you. Things that you don't even know yourself. It also lets me put new thoughts and feelings into you, so you can experience them without being there."

Anna thought for a few moments. "What is Shawn?"

"Shawn is exactly like you. He just doesn't have a body."

Anna didn't fully understand but nodded. She wondered for a few moments. Then she touched her lips with her paw. "Where did we come from?"

Isidore frowned. "What do you mean?"

"I mean, I came from my mother. And she came for her mother. But where did the first mother come from?"

"Ah." Isidore understood. "Well, man built an amazing machine. They are called many things, but you can think of them as the Mother Creator, because it is the mother who gives birth to the child. But we refer to them as *they* and *them* because they really are both the mother and the father at the same time."

Anna shook her head. "But... if the mother and the father have the same blood, the child will be weak and sick. It will die!"

"It is much, much more complicated than that," Isidore said with a sigh. "But—okay. Let me try to explain it this way. There are certain plants: if you break a twig off them and stick it in the ground, another one will grow. You can do this any number of times and none of them will be weak and sick."

Anna covered her lips with her paw. She nodded slowly.

"Anyway, so the Mother Creator can make any kind of mammal. They make them from a special paste. The Mother Creator is powerful, but they can only do what man tells them to do. In the beginning, man asked them to make all kinds of mammalæ—from here and from faraway lands. Mammalæ that neither you nor I have ever seen.

"They were sent to live all over the world. Their jobs were always to be our helpers. I heard that one day, after a long voyage to Russia, a ship carrying arctic foxes, wolves and bears ran aground. Your earliest ancestors escaped from the wreck. Since then, you have lived in the woods in one of the coldest, most desolate places on earth. And thrived. Man tried to wipe you out but could not, so they started hunting you for fun instead.

"As time went on," he continued, "man told Mother Creator to take away your ability to have children. They told them to stop making mammalæ that are not from this land. Foxes, Wolves, Raccoons, Ferrets—they called them *exotics*—slowly started dying out. Only a handful remain today."

"That is so sad!" said Anna. "How do you know all this?"

"I helped build the Mother Creator," said Isidore. He sounded angry. "I helped to create a special language so that they could speak to us, and us to them. It lets man explain to them exactly what kind of mammal they want to make." He gave a small sigh. "They got rid of me once my work was done.

And because of their NDAs and other corporate bullshit, I haven't had a stable job since."

Anna looked at Isidore. *"If he helped create the Mother Creator,"* she thought, *"he must be some kind of god himself!*

"Why do you not call her on the television?" Anna asked after thinking for a bit.

"She is not on the Intern—um—she is trapped inside SFA's building. She cannot speak to anyone on the outside. And no-one can speak in. The only way to speak to her is to visit her. And I will never be allowed to do that again." Isidore looked up at another one of his displays. He seemed happy with the symbols. He leaned to his right and typed on the other device. It was the one he used in her room, the one with a panel and a keyboard in one. Isidore had already shown her his other machines. They were noisy and ugly, but Anna thought this one was cute.

"What is that?" asked Anna, pointing.

"This is my portable," he said. "It can do most of the things the rest of the machines can do, but it is smaller, and I can carry it around. I also use it to see what my bigger, stronger machines are doing."

"What are you doing with it now?" she asked.

"There are some bad people looking for us. I wanted to make sure I have everything in one place so we can take it along when we leave."

Isidore didn't want to spook Anna, but he knew that every minute they remained at his apartment, they were in danger. Shawn was in hibernation. The MæSIM was powered down. He was now only a stream of bits on secondary storage; one solar flare or a bad fall away from disappearing forever. The MæSIM was a full-sized blade. It was bulky and heavy. It was not meant to be carried around. Isidore had to use the wheeled, padded suitcase it first arrived in to lug it. If he only had mammal.img, he could have easily created a virtual machine on his portable and everything would be in one place—even if it would be a bit sluggish. No such luck. He emptied his cupboards and picked through the clothes on the floor. He stuffed some of them into another wheeled suitcase. He packed his toiletries and his tablet, too. "Here," he said, tossing Anna a cotton sack with a rope sling.

She sniffed the bag and opened it up. There were four plastic bottles of water, a packet of mammal snacks, and an extra change of clothes inside. "Thank you," she said with a smile.

There was a chime. Isidore fumbled for his tablet. He was relieved to see a chubby man with worn blue jeans outside. "Who is it?" he asked through the door, just to be one hundred percent sure. "Buffalo Bill's moving services."

"Come inside."

A stocky black man stepped in, followed close behind by two muscular buffalo in blue overalls. All three had the moving company's logo on their chests. One of the buffalo carried a bundle of cardboard boxes, while the other dragged a small foldable trolley behind him. They nodded at Isidore. "Take everything," said Isidore, pointing to the space behind him. "Just leave the computer equipment and the displays. I'll let you know when you can bring my stuff back from storage."

"Sure," said the man, now turning towards his helpers. "Fellows. Get busy!"

"And," Isidore added, "give the place a *thorough* scrub. I don't want any hair or fur left."

Bill nodded. "Will do." As the buffalo started emptying his kitchen cupboards, Isidore dragged his suitcases to the front door.

"Why are they taking all your things?" Anna asked.

"I want to hide our scents," he explained. "But I have to leave my computers so I can still work on them when I'm away." She clearly did not understand, but he didn't have time to explain. He took a last, longing place at his home, sighed, and put a hat over his bald head. "Anna," he said. Her ears perked up. "Come. Bring your bag. We are going for a walk."

Isidore's clothes were soaked with sweat. He breathed shallowly and fast. The suitcases he dragged behind him felt like anvils. He could only imagine how Anna was feeling. They walked in the shadows and through subways as much as they could and rested long and often. They drank copious amounts of water. The bottles they carried with them only lasted about three quarters of the way. Beach Road ran alongside a wide promenade bordering the ocean. There were many people basking on the artificial grass. Without exception, they hid beneath gazebos and small tents to block out most of the sun's deadly rays. There was a strong salty smell, carried from the ocean by a breeze. Motorcars and motorcycles whizzed past.

Just when it felt like he could walk no more, they came to a tall coastal modern-style residential building. It was tall, light, and newly built. They entered the lobby and immediately sat down on two of the many seats along the wall. There was an android behind the reception desk. Its lifeless eyes scanned them and gave a wanting stare. "Welcome," it said. "Are you visiting one of our residents?"

"One—moment—" Isidore heaved, his chest on his knees, sweat dripping on the floor. Anna was hyperventilating too, with her tongue hanging from the side of her mouth.

"You appear to be in distress, miss," said the android in a voice emulating concern. "Would you like me to call an ambulance?"

"No," she replied. "I—just need—to—sit."

It took Isidore about five minutes to catch his breath. He stood up, leaving Anna and his suitcases behind. "We're here to see Catherine Blake."

Catherine's apartment was cool and airy. She had given both a dose of electrolytes and a glass of ice-cold water to cool them down. They lay back on couches in her living room with their chins up and their legs parted. Isidore had taken off his t-shirt, and Anna had a wet towel over her head. The space was grand and fresh. The kitchen—about double the size of Isidore's living area—was separated from the living area by a wide granite surface. Everything was shiny. The light fixtures on the tall ceilings were made of soft, textured glass. Her television was huge. There was a balcony at the far end of the living room that overlooked the ocean. It was closed off by an edgeless glass door that let in ample natural light. Her apartment was big enough for a family of four.

"To what do I owe the pleasure of your company?" joked Catherine as she poured boiling water into a pot. "And also... what on earth made you decide to walk here?"

"SFA is onto us," said Isidore. "We needed to leave my apartment immediately. You were the only one we could trust—and within walking distance. I wanted to make sure we covered our tracks. There's no other way to get here without tapping."

"You are lucky," she said as she stirred. "I was about to go out to the gym." Catherine sat down by Anna with a large cup of tea in her hand. "How are you doing Anna? The walk here must have been awful. Are your paws ok?"

"They burned," replied Anna, "but I feel better. Thank you."

Catherine knew Anna was telling the truth. There was life in her eyes now. Catherine smiled. "We'll take care of your paws," she assured. "I've got some very good salves for that. Anna, you can sleep in the bedroom second to your left." She pointed. "It's got a floor mattress. Isidore, you can set up your equipment across the passage from her—" she winked, "and you can sleep with me."

"A strange thing happened," said Shawn as they strolled through the forest together looking for food. "I felt very sleepy yesterday morning, so I decided to take a nap in my tent. When I woke up, it was morning again. I could swear that I slept an entire day. And I wasn't even tired to begin with!"

Anna frowned. "That is strange!"

Catherine stood with folded arms. She watched the console over her lover's shoulder. As the veterinarian, she was more interested in the two foxes' vitals than the content of their conversations, or what they did. "He's definitely taken to her," said Catherine with a nod. "Those hormones are telling."

"What about her?" asked Isidore, switching the console to her. "She likes him," said Catherine. "But she's not quite ready to give herself to him yet. This might change when she goes into heat."

Isidore swallowed. "Do you know when that might be?"

"From her hormone levels, it could be any day now. But," she was quick to add, "I'm sure by now you know not to rush things. Let nature do its thing."

"I wouldn't dream of interfering," he said with a smile. "Now," said Catherine, "since we are on the topic of hormones…"

She wet her lips.

Later that afternoon when they were all having lunch together, there was an alarm. Isidore dropped his cutlery in his plate, pulled out of his chair, and ran to fetch his tablet. He cursed as he emerged from the passage, his eyes on the display. "Not a moment too soon," he grumbled. Anna frowned. Catherine looked on with concern. "Cast the feed to the living room television," he commanded. "Show camera three in the center frame."

The television obliged. Anna gasped, and Catherine folded her arms. There stood a robotic creature in Isidore's living room. Its shape resembled that of a very skinny human. Dull grey elastic covered its mechanical insides. It didn't look friendly. Its legs were long and thin with tiny rubber pads for feet. The creature had some sensors at the top of its torso, but it did not resemble a head. Its hands were a complicated mess of fingers and sensors. *"How did that thing get into my apartment?"* Switching cameras, Isidore could see that the front door was closed and still intact. "It must have hacked its way in."

Anna's ears perked up. Everyone kept quiet and listened. There was a faint whirring of servos and the tiny squeaks of rubber feet on the floor. The three watched in horror as the creature methodically opened every cupboard and drawer in the kitchen. Then the bathroom. Then the bedrooms. It examined, scanned, and took pictures. There wasn't much to see. Having finished exploring the rest of the apartment, it decided to enter the study. Isidore boiled with anger. The machine had entered his sacred space. "The fucking nerve!" he cursed. "This. Stops. Now!" He dashed to fetch his portable and started furiously hammering away at the keyboard. Catherine's eyes followed the symbols on his console. Anna's eyes were locked onto the television where the creature now looked underneath Isidore's desk. The furious typing stopped suddenly with the loud clack of the enter key. Isidore closed his eyes and took a deep breath.

Catherine smiled. "I guess that's why you became the computer programmer. And I became the vet!"

"Same core modules," he said. Isidore kept his portable on his lap and turned his eyes to Catherine's television. The android located the network switch. It produced a connector from its finger and slotted it into one of the vacant ports. As expected, the creature tried to make an inventory of his systems. Red text flashed on each of the many displays: *"Access denied."* A small progress bar on Isidore's portable quickly slid to hundred percent. He smiled. "Two can play your game, USC. Just you wait!"

The video feed stopped. "The thing discovered that we are looking," Isidore explained. "It killed our feed. It's now going to try and break into my other systems again."

"What happens now?" asked Catherine.

"Give it a moment," he smirked. Anna's ears perked up. The feed returned suddenly, but now it was a single pane of video with a markedly different perspective. The image was wide-angled and there were large black triangles at the top and bottom center. It was a panoramic image, fed directly from the android's cameras.

"Clever," remarked Catherine as she nodded. "You've just hijacked yourself a 'bot. What are you going to do now?"

"I'm going to have some fun." Isidore popped his knuckles and settled comfortably in his seat. He set down his portable on the floor and pulled out his tablet. He slid his fingers over the device. The android started moving. It unplugged itself, then turned around and proceeded to the door of the apartment. It stepped outside and gently closed the door behind it. It then walked over to a small red box by the lifts, looked back to make sure one of the building's security cameras was trained on it, then smashed it to pieces. A siren wailed and lights flashed along the passage. Anna covered her ears.

Isidore slid and tapped the tablet some more. The android hurried down the stairs. The stairwell on the lower floors was already filling up. The machine shoved people and mammalæ aside to escape. In the street below, bodies spilled out of the building. Marshals in bright yellow jackets—not even fastened yet—tried to herd them across the road to safety. Traffic had stopped. Motorcars hooted and people shouted. Chaos.

The android broke free from the crowd and took a jog further down the road and turned right. It crossed without looking. A car slammed to a stop with screeching tires. The android turned around, looked at the driver with contempt, and smashed his windshield and kicked off his mirror. In the distance there were sirens. The android ran past the railway station and the castle, onto the highway. It was not long until a squad of police officers were in pursuit in car and on motorcycle. The android glanced back over its shoulder, then jumped the median to double back against traffic. Tires screeched. A car slammed into the back of another. A third hit them from behind. Soon the highway was gridlocked. Angry drivers stood outside their vehicles, gesturing with their fists and shouting. The police parked behind them and gave chase on foot. The android smashed some more cars.

When Isidore got tired of the shenanigans, he made the android bolt towards the edge of the unfinished overpass. It stopped right before the edge and looked down, as if contemplating its fate. It did the android equivalent of mooning the police, then turned towards them. The officers were ready to immobilize it with a microwave cannon and live ammunition. The machine raised its arms, but not in surrender. It dove backwards to the parking lot below. As an encore, it crashed through the roof of a stationary bus. The transmission ended and switched back to the feed of the apartment.

The look on Isidore's face was priceless. He set down the tablet, stretched his arms, and let out a satisfactory yawn.

"They are going to be very, very angry," said Catherine.

"What happened?" asked Anna.

It was another late-night comms session. Jeanne was conflicted as to whether she should laugh. The lab behind her was a buzz of activity as before. On the other end of the Atlantic sat Michelle, the head of PR, the CTO, and one of the directors. They all sat in a boardroom—all of them were miserable.

"Things didn't exactly go to plan, did they?" said Jeanne. She tried very hard to sound disappointed.

"It's an absolute disaster!" roared PR.

"I've fired every worm in the comms team for this!" barked the CTO.

"Maybe you understand now why we stick with our Mammalæ," Jeanne said. "Androids lack the *human touch*—and they cannot be controlled remotely," she was quick to add. Michelle's face was red with embarrassment. "I'll leave you to mend your public relations problems," Jeanne said. "I can only imagine the collateral."

"I want blood," shouted the director, slamming his fists on the table.

"You'll have your blood," Jeanne assured with a smile. She looked beside her and gestured to someone off camera to step closer. A large leopard male stepped into the frame. Its face was hard and expressionless. It was about as tall as her, but its muscular body completely dwarfed her own. The USC staff did a double take. "I'd like to introduce you to FEL9," said Jeanne. "He's now fully formed and ready to be programmed."

"Oh. My. God," said Michelle, for the first time in the call showing anything except anger on her face. "Isn't that... overkill?"

"Perhaps," said Jeanne, upturning her hands. "But we here at SFA believe in doing things properly. More than likely when they see our muscle, that little fox and her thief will simply surrender. But even if they don't... we'll catch them. We'll settle this matter the old-fashioned way. The way nature intended. Claw-to-back and maw-to-neck."

FEL9

Two days later, the chamber that held the capsule decompressed with a hiss. FEL9's handler left his luggage inside. He squeezed past the other nineteen passengers, to leave the small hatch first. Not a moment too soon. He hunched over the nearest trash can and lost his lunch.

"Got the 'loopies'?" joked a fellow passenger in a business suit as he patted Handler on the back.

FEL9 stepped out with the rest of the passengers, lugging the two heavy suitcases behind him as if they weighed nothing. The leopard's imposing frame made the capsule look small. He stretched his back and popped his neck, taking a deep sniff at his new surroundings.

FEL9 wore a light brown uniform with short sleeves and matching shorts. They were airy and movable. He didn't seem affected by the grueling forty-minute trip. Handler managed to compose himself after a while, and they left the tube station together. "We'll drop our bags at the hotel," he said. "We'll meet up with the private investigator. Then we'll go to their last known location." The leopard nodded.

They were about to hail an Autotaxi when they were stopped by two mammalæ control officers. "Good afternoon," one of them said. "Mind if we scan you?"

FEL9's upper lip twitched. Handler exchanged an angry glance with him. The big cat extended his enormous paw.

Beep

"FEL9," she said, but then did a double take. She frowned deeply as she examined her device more closely. *"Redacted Type?"* She turned towards her partner, showing him the readout.

He scratched his head. "Special purpose. This is a first. What does this mean?"

Handler produced his tab and showed them a document with an official SFA letterhead. He then invited them to scan him. The officers' eyes were wide. "It means," he said, "we are here on official SFA business. You should stop wasting our time and let us carry on with our work!" FEL9's upper lip lifted again, showing the side of his fang. The officers nodded and backed away.

"Have a good day, sir."

Handler and FEL9 didn't greet them back.

Catherine stacked the dishwasher. "Can I get you something else Anna?" she asked.

"No thank you, miss Catherine."

Isidore sat in the living room. He replayed the video of the android in his apartment on the television. Unlike the first time, he was now completely focused and examined every little detail of the intrusion—just in case he may have missed something. Anna stood on the balcony, gazing over the ocean.

"See anything interesting yet?" Catherine asked.

"I only see one thing that worries me," Isidore said. "Look." He paused the frame where the android stood in the bathroom. In the cupboard above the sink, it had seen something of interest. It paused and took out a small white bottle of pills the movers must have missed. The machine examined the label carefully and put it back. "It means they have a causal link between Anna and your veterinary practice."

"I wouldn't worry too much," said Catherine with a shrug. "I see a lot of mammalæ every week."

Isidore's tablet chimed as they were having dinner that evening. He grabbed it and immediately cast the contents to the television set. They watched and saw an empty living area, but there was loud banging at the door.

There was another. And another. And another. Then a pause.

The door opened inwards, and the lights turned on. A leopard and a scrawny man entered.

"Lord. That thing is huge!" said Isidore, his fist to his mouth. Anna didn't say anything, but her tail was drawn between her legs. "I wasn't expecting them to be here so soon," muttered Isidore. "They must have pumped that thing full of growth hormones... and done the *absolute* minimum programming to get him here so quickly." They kept watching the feed.

FEL9's handler moped around aimlessly. He made a half-hearted attempt to look for clues. FEL9 was determined but hard-pawed. He walked around the empty rooms, sniffing every corner. He would be lucky to pick up anything in the sterilized space. When he did not find anything in the living room, the bathroom, the bedrooms, nor the kitchen, the big cat grumbled. He entered the study and examined the floor. He sniffed the table. He then ducked behind that computer rack, where he remained for a few moments. The hairs on Isidore's neck stood on end.

The leopard emerged with a clump of fuzz, no larger than a man's thumbprint. He must have taken it from one of the system's still-spinning fans! *"Shit."* He dropped the sample into a small glass bottle and sealed the lid. Isidore entered a command on his portable. FEL9's attention was immediately drawn to one of the monitors that lit up. On its surface was an elaborate grid of black patterns on a white background.

"MT293E7453235519FM," the leopard said.

"4725120453235319RM," said Anna at nearly the same time.

Catherine quickly stepped up and placed her hands over Anna's eyes.

"Red... Green... Red... Yellow..." the leopard said. On hearing this, the handler stumbled down the passage. He ran as if he was on fire. The leopard was still mesmerized. His eyes still scanned the display from right to left, and he was about to say more things. The handler grabbed one of Isidore's keyboards and smashed the display to pieces.

"He did not absorb everything," Isidore grumbled. "Dammit!"

"Fuck!" the handler cursed as he gasped for his breath.

"What?" grunted the leopard, now back in the present.

"Nothing. Just—nothing!"

FEL9 poked around Isidore's broken keyboard on the desk. Amongst the scattered keys and the broken circuit boards until he found a tiny scrap of gunk. He placed this in another container and sealed it. "I will sniff these when we leave," the leopard said. "This place stinks."

On hearing this, Isidore fell back into the couch, tossed his head backwards, and groaned. "I guess we were naive to think we could completely erase ourselves. I never thought of the fans. Or the keyboards."

"At least you have his serial," said Catherine.

Isidore nodded. "We know what those miscreants look like. But... they have Anna's scent. And mine too. They already know what we look like. It's fair game now."

"On that note, Isidore," said Catherine with folded arms, "you and Anna are going to have to move along. I don't mind keeping you, but I can't risk them implicating me in this." Isidore nodded.

"I understand." He was now on his portable, picking the beast's serial number apart. "Ok," he said.

```
Manufactured Mammal, 1st Generation
Panthera Pardus Anomalis (Mammalæous)
Serial Number MT293E7453235519FM
MæOS 2.9.1.4.0000001 Patch 002.09.511, Rev. 5
Type Redacted
```

"What do the other flags say?" asked Catherine.

> **Red** - Not able to deliberately injure or kill humans.
>
> **Green** - Able to deliberately injure or kill other mammalæ, if requested by the imprinted person or if otherwise necessary for its own survival.
>
> **Red** - Not authorized to carry or use any weapons.

`Yellow` - Limited autonomy when the imprinted person is not present.

"Sadly, that's all we got. I had about fifty other semaphores lined up, if that stupid handler did not stop him. I wish the interface wasn't so slow." He turned to Catherine. "We don't really have many options. We need to get Anna as far away from this place as we can. They won't leave until they have her. I am going to see what our options are." A few minutes later, Isidore looked up from his tablet. "There's a tube to Johannesburg. It lines up nicely with a high-speed train to the northern border. It departs tomorrow at around lunchtime. If we can get to that pod, we may be able to give them the slip."

Handler and FEL9 were now checked into a cheap hotel in town. There were two single beds on the carpeted floor, a desk with a chair and a television, a coffee station, and a bathroom. The place smelled moldy, and the view through the waist-high window was unspectacular—that of another building. Handler opened the largest of the two suitcases on his bed as FEL9 paced up and down. Inside was a thick layer of padding with various cut-outs. There were some drones, a bundle of zip-ties, a chip scanner, and a pocket-sized tranquilizer gun. Handler slid the gun into a shoulder-strap holster under his shirt. He stashed the zip-ties and the scanner in his pockets. He then removed the drones from the case, one by one, checked comms with his tablet, walked to the window, and tossed the whirring devices into the wind. After he had done so, he turned to the leopard.

"Let's take a walk."

Anna and Shawn took shelter in his tent. Rain poured down in the woods. The fire had washed out, and the smell was that of smoldering wood and leaves. They sat beside one another. Anna rested her head on Shawn's shoulder. He held his arm around her waist, and their other paws were woven in their laps. "A man and a leopard are hunting us."

"What's a leopard?"

"It is a terrible thing," Anna said. "It is a big, scary mammal with a yellow coat and black-and-brown spots. It has huge, sharp fangs and claws. It looks so strong and fast!"

"I'm so scared something is going to happen to you," said Shawn. "I just want to be there to protect you."

She sighed. "Me too, Shawn."

The two foxes sat quietly, staring at the darkness and the rain outside.

Isidore was perplexed. "I have no idea how this is," he said, observing the foxes' conversation. "They are clearly in love now. There are no societal norms that prevent them from doing so... Why are they not having sex yet?"

"They think about relationships differently than we do," said Catherine, who watched with her hand on his shoulder. "For them it's about forming strong bonds. They don't just have sex for fun like we do. Their goal is to mate and have kits. This can't happen if she is not in heat. They are waiting it out."

Isidore sighed, rubbing his temples. "I'm starting to think this entire project was a complete waste of my time. I have nothing to show, and our lives are in danger."

Catherine kneeled behind him and rubbed his shoulders. "You are ten times the man you were when this all started. And I'm convinced you will break the code." She paused. "Even though I don't know what you plan to do with it. That's a different conversation. But cheer up. I believe in you. I know you will do the right thing. Your breakthrough will come." She gave him a little bite on his earlobe. "Leave Anna with her sweetheart for a little while. Let them bond." She then flung her hair back. "Come. Let's go do some very naughty things in my bedroom before the big journey starts."

It was the home stretch. The tube station was just across the street. This time, Isidore made no attempt to cover his tracks. He wanted to lure them away from Catherine's apartment and into the bowels of the city. She had dropped them off by a cheap hotel, not too far from where he lived. They walked to the tube station from there. Unlike the main railway station—which was sprawling and still had an old-fashioned charm about it—the tube station was compact and state-of-the-art. There was one ticketing station and two gates, one for arrivals and one for departures. Large displays showed the status of the line and proudly advertised the maximum speed attained during the day—and over the system's life. It clocked in around twice the speed of sound.

The smell was that of food. "I am hungry," said Anna as they made their way to a seating area.

"Rather don't eat anything now," he replied.

"Why?"

"The tube isn't for the faint-hearted," he explained, "It can make you really, really sick." The name of their pod now showed on the large display above the entry gate: express service to Johannesburg. It was fifteen minutes prior to boarding—it would be a long fifteen minutes.

Isidore read the news on his tablet and Anna rested with her eyes closed. Little did they know a pair of tiny lenses had already zoomed in on them and were sending signals to a tablet, just across the road.

Five minutes before departure, he and Anna rose and stretched their backs. So close.

Suddenly there was a shrill siren and flashing lights all around. Anna jumped. The text on the boards above the gates changed to show a message in bright red with white lettering: "Attention! Attention!" called a voice loudly. "There has been an unspecified threat against this facility. All persons are to leave the station immediately and assemble on the roadway opposite the terminus. Security staff will assess the situation and confirm when re-entry is safe. Attention! Attention!"

"I don't like this," Isidore said. "This is way too coincidental. Stay close!" They filtered through the gathering and tried to blend in, but there weren't many bodies, and Anna's white coat was difficult to hide. A small drone whirred above their heads and seemed to focus in on them. Isidore heard and saw this. He looked up briefly and swallowed.

"Anna, Run!"

He dropped his regular suitcase, only hanging onto his equipment. They forced a path through the crowd as the small nuisance tracked them from above. They heard a mighty roar. Glancing back, Isidore nearly fell. Coming towards them was the hulking leopard they had seen the previous day. Isidore grabbed Anna's paw. They dashed over a road, sending cross-traffic screeching to a halt. A streetcar lazily pulled into a stop just ahead of them. "Jump!" He leapt through the closing door, causing it to snap open again. His heavy suitcase hopped on his heels, and Anna jumped in too. They tapped hand and paw on the yellow reader by the entrance. It beeped. The door locks engaged, and the car started moving forward.

Looking through the rear window, they saw the monster follow them on paw. The tiny drone followed them, too. Its cameras poked through the side-window, and as much as the duo tried to hide behind other passengers, it kept them in frame. The car wasn't crowded. Other passengers were alarmed by their strange behavior.

"Are you okay?" asked a dog.

"Do you want me to call the police?" asked its owner.

"We're... fine. It was just a misunderstanding. We'll be... fine," said Isidore.

They were panicking. The streetcar moved way too slowly. It outpaced the leopard when cruising, but each time it stopped he gained ground again. There was no sign of the leopard getting tired or slowing down. Isidore's knuckles were white as he clung to the pole. His eyes were anchored on the road behind. There was a long straight where they made good ground, but the streetcar made an extended stop when several passengers wanted to get out.

The doors opened slowly. He sweated bullets. The big cat came within paces of the door. There was a look of terror on Anna's face. The doors closed moments before FEL9 could board. He hammered against the door and dragged his claws across the glass windows with an awful screech, but he had missed the port of call, and the heavy streetcar didn't acknowledge him. It slid forward again. FEL9 ran right beside them now. His eyes were on Anna's. He bared his teeth, eliciting alarmed looks from the other passengers. He suddenly stopped and fell out of sight as the streetcar ducked into a dark tunnel, bypassing the gridlock at the intersection of Bree, Buitengracht, and Strand Streets.

Isidore's breath heaved. "That—was—too close," he said.

Their freedom hung by a thread. The tunnel was short. The vehicle would soon be at grade again, just beyond the stadium. And they could not get off anywhere in between. Isidore struggled to steady his hands. He scrambled to make a call from his tablet in the darkness. "We need an Autotaxi. ASAP!"

The streetcar had hardly left the tunnel when Isidore slammed the stop button. He dragged Anna and his suitcase from the door. There stood a white hatchback with the Autotaxi logo on its side.

Isidore tapped his hand on the yellow pad by the door, and the rear doors unlocked. They leapt in and slammed them shut. The taxi pulled off. Behind them drifted a tiny drone. *"Where would you like me to take you?"* asked the taxi.

"Take us to the underground parking near the Golden Acre mall. I'll give further instructions when we are there."

"No problem. Standard waiting rates will apply." With the vehicle now moving, Isidore took a moment to catch his breath. There was a whine around them as the driverless vehicle took lazy turns through the city streets.

Isidore was on his tablet again. "Rick!" he said, "Man, I'm glad to see you. Listen, we have a crisis. I will explain later. I need to know something: do you still have rooms available at the convention?"

Rick's eyes twinkled behind the screen. "Sure thing, Saint! Would you like to room with anyone in particular?"

"I need a private room. For me and Anna. Single or double. I don't care. Any floor. But it must be in the main hotel."

"Hmmm, sure. I'll tell the hotel to release one of the VIP rooms. One of the lower-downs are going to have to sleep in the overflow. Anything else you need?"

"I also need you to book us in. I don't want me or Anna to be on the hotel register or the convention systems."

"That's a big ask, Saint. We could get into trouble for that. Give me a minute and I'll see what I can do."

There was no sight of the drone now as they ducked into the underground parking, but it had their license plates. It could still find them. They had to jump ship. He and Anna sat in silence as vehicles and pedestrians moved in the murky space.

Isidore's tablet vibrated and sprang to life. "Meet me at the VIP registration desk."

"Arrange for another Autotaxi to pick us up at Salt River Station," commanded Isidore.

"Are you not happy with our service? Would you like to speak with a customer service representative?" the taxi asked.

"No. We are taking the Metrorail from here."

After getting out, the duo pressed through the crowd, past stalls selling Cape Malay food, tech gadgets, and plastic trinkets. They took a brief walk under the roadway to the station. With any luck, they'd shaken their pursuers. After five minutes, they boarded the train bound for the southern suburbs. Two stops down the line, they got into another Autotaxi.

[################....] 80%

The Convention

He was sure that they had shaken off the drone. On the highway now, they drove past a colossal glass and concrete building to their left. The taxi slowed down as they entered city traffic. A twist. A left turn. They entered a large courtyard, where the taxi pulled up to a bright and airy, glass-covered entrance.

Isidore got out first. He scanned the air around them for a small, buzzing hell-device but did not see or hear one.

Humans and mammalæ stood around the entrance. Some were vaping. Others were simply soaking the atmosphere or each other's company. There were other vehicles behind them. Isidore unloaded his suitcase and gestured for Anna to follow closely. They stepped into the grand entrance. The interior was cool, the floors were clean porcelain, and the ceilings were high. It was a typical building from the early 21st century. All over the floor stood large rolodex posters, and against the walls were unmoving television displays. On each was the picture of a proud, little springbok mammal. "Wel—coming all—Visitor?" Anna tried her best to read. Isidore nodded and smiled.

They came to another sign of the little springbok with an outstretched hoof, directing the attendees to the registration desks. There was a long line of visitors who waited for their turn to scan in and collect their welcome packs. Even though the wait would be long, there was a sense of excitement. A sense of camaraderie. Some chatted. Others hugged and scratched each other behind the ears. There were humans. There were mammalæ... and there were also humans dressed up like mammalæ.

"What... are those?" Anna asked, pointing.

"I'll explain later. Just follow and stay close. We need to get to our room."

Isidore saw what he was looking for. There was an inconspicuous side-room. The friendly springbok poster by the door now held its hoof in the air. The speech bubble said, "VIP Registration Only." They entered. A man and a woman sat behind a pop-up table with two tablets on top, scanning visitors from a much shorter line.

Behind them, looking very smug, stood a human in a mammal suit. He was a stubby, green and white fox with a big smile and slight belly. "Hey Saint! Welcome!" he said as he recognized his friend. He opened his fuzzy green arms to give him a hug. The green fox's emerald eyes sparkled. They blinked realistically and his mouth moved more-or-less naturally when he spoke.

Anna stared at him with a gaping maw.

"Meet my friend, Rick," Isidore said.

Anna nodded. Rick reached out to her. She looked at Isidore, uncertain of what to do. Isidore nodded. She reluctantly reached out to him. His soft—but giant—paw squeezed hers gently. Rick turned back to the registration desk and assured them that they would register later, once they dropped their bags.

"What are your shirt sizes?" asked the woman behind the table.

"Extra small and Large."

They were both handed large paper bags filled with merchandise. Rick escorted them across a short, glass sky-bridge to the hotel lobby. The decor was modern and stylish. The porcelain floor was covered in a thick, soft carpet. There were clusters of benches where various patrons sat socializing.

"I've booked the room in my name. I've checked in," explained Rick as they walked. "We can go there now."

The elevator was crammed full of bodies. Not once or twice, a buzzer and a small display indicated that it was overloaded, and some of the passengers had to get out. The crowd mumbled and gazed in admiration as they saw Rick. A couple or patrons complimented his new suit. Some stepped out respectfully to let him and his guests climb aboard. The elevator started to move.

Many passengers gawked at Anna. Isidore could see this made her very uncomfortable. A person in a suit tried to affectionately scratch Anna behind the ears, at which she snarled, showing her tiny canines at them. Isidore glared and asked the person politely not to *molest* his comfort mammal. They quickly apologized and looked the other way.

The elevator took them somewhere half-way up the towering block. They stepped out into a luxuriously appointed passage. It was quieter than the lobby but still bubbled with excited conversation. There were only a handful of other guests. Some cleverly opted to go down the stairwell instead of the overcrowded lifts. There were many doors. Outside some of the doors stood stacks of empty pizza boxes. Anna licked her chops.

A short walk down, they stopped. Rick tapped them into a room. The space inside was slightly smaller than Isidore's apartment—but much more luxurious. The floor was laid out with smooth faux-wood tiles. The space smelled of lavender and coffee. There was a small kitchen and a door that led to a bathroom. After setting down his bag, Isidore plopped down on the freshly made bed with heaving breath. "Thanks Rick."

"Sure thing, Saint. Now you got to tell me what's going on."

"We are being chased by the corporation. They are in town, and they have sent a dangerous leopard after us. We can't go home. I thought the best place to disappear would be at the largest gathering of mammalæ in the southern hemisphere."

"That makes sense," Rick said, nodding. "But this is worrying. I'll ask the convention staff to keep a lookout. We'll be able to stall them. Do you have the leopard's serial number?"

"I do. I'll give it to you now."

"We'll deny them entry. And we'll tab you when they try."

"That's my side of the bargain," he said, "But now you got to promise me you won't do anything stupid. As a convention chair, I have a reputation to protect."

"I'll do my best."

"Next point of order—um—" said Isidore, "I dropped my clothes when we were being chased. All I have are the clothes I'm wearing now. And they stink. I can wash my underwear in the basin and I have this convention shirt, but I'll need new pants."

Rick's eyes twinkled. "I have just the solution for that! Hang on." He left the room.

Meanwhile Anna sniffed around. She found a small packet of mammal treats in a bowl by the coffee machine. She licked her chops and emptied its contents into her maw. She helped herself to some water from the faucet in the bathroom. Isidore took a Blast from the mini-bar and fed his brain. A few minutes later, Rick returned. He plopped a large suitcase down on the small space by the television. When he opened it up, Isidore retched. It was Rick's old fur suit. The one-piece body was made of ultra-ventilated faux fur with an uncanny resemblance to the coat of a jackal, but vibrant, sparkling blue. The head was slightly oversized.

"Take a shower. Suit up!" Rick invited. "We have a VIP dinner tonight—I'd really love for the two of you to join us. Give it some thought, will you? Got to go. I have some other VIP guests to welcome." Isidore nodded. "Oh, and missus," Rick said, addressing Anna directly for the first time, "I just want to say. You are beautiful. And you are very welcome at our convention!"

Anna smiled awkwardly. "Thank you, sir," she said.

Rick handed them an old-fashioned keycard. He closed the door on his way out and left them alone. Isidore finished his drink and took some chips from the mini-bar. He shared these with Anna. After that he took a long, hot shower. He layered himself with some of Rick's musky-smelling deodorant that he had also borrowed. "Sorry Anna." He then climbed into the suit. Anna helped him zip in up at the back. He slipped on the head. It was kitted out with an on-board computer that took care of peripheral vision, facial expression matching, and the like. It booted automatically the moment he put it on. The flabby fabric around his middle was the only indication that the suit was not made for him.

Anna glared at his disproportionate head, his body and his faux digitigrade legs. She gave a little laugh.

"This is not funny," he grumbled. "These people are fucked in their heads." He removed the head and placed it on the kitchen table.

"What is happening in this place?" Anna asked.

He rolled his eyes and sighed. "It's a big gathering of people who *like* mammalæ. People who *like* them *way too much.* It's their religion. They celebrate everything mammalæ. They draw pictures. They play games. They wear these crazy suits and pretend to be mammalæ themselves."

"That does not make sense—" said Anna, "but they seem very nice."

"Right?" said Isidore, upturning his hands. "Which reminds me. We are going to need to get you a disguise."

After a brief catch-up with their private investigator, Handler and FEL9 left their hotel. They took an Autotaxi to the convention center and fell into the registration line, which now snaked halfway along the lobby. FEL9 glanced at the cheerful humans in their silly suits. Every now and then he took a deep sniff, as if the vixen would somehow walk into his paws. When they finally reached the front, they were both miserable.

"We are here for the convention," said Handler to a human in a ferret suit.

"Did you pre-book?" they asked.

"No."

"There aren't any rooms available in the hotel, but I could give you and your mammal week passes?"

Handler nodded.

"Will you tap in for me please?" Beep. "Sir," they said. "It says here you have been permanently banned from attending this convention."

FEL9 showed his teeth. Handler gaped in disbelief. "What? How?!"

A member of convention security stood by with pepper spray in his hand. He shook the canister. "Sorry, that's what the system says," they repeated. "Next please!"

"Wait!" cried Handler. "Is there someone we can talk to?"

"Not right now, sir. All senior convention staff are busy getting the venue ready. We can take your details and ask them to make contact?"

"It's fine," he cursed. "Just—just leave it!" They turned away and left the building.

Isidore's tablet buzzed as they gorged themselves on their second helping of bland room service food. He quickly lifted his device as he chewed. He swallowed. "They're here."

Handler was pissed off. He and FEL9 wandered in the streets around the convention center. Everything seemed so... normal. There was asphalt. Dying trees. Wandering pedestrians and cars. The distant bell of a streetcar. The enormous television screen on the side of the streaming media services building. "They are here," said Handler as he gritted his teeth. "There's no other reason why they won't let us in!" He looked at FEL9. "If only you weren't so fucking stupid to blurt out your serial number!" FEL9 growled. Handler tensed. "Easy now, big boy. Let's go back to our hotel. I've set the drones to monitor all exits. They can't leave."

Anna had never seen such a thing. There was a wall of bodies in front of them, and there were too many scents and smells to count.

"Beautiful, isn't it?" said Rick.

Isidore just nodded. Anna was sure she heard him sigh beneath the jackal head. "Remember," Isidore said, "We are only here to get Anna a disguise. Nothing else."

"I know just the thing," said Rick. "There's a coloring booth... over... there! I know the owner. They always do excellent work."

Anna was anxious as they moved through the crowd. She was much smaller than everyone else, and she was scared that she would get lost. They came to a stall with a bright green sign and a tiny table. There was a tablet showing pictures of mammalæ and humans with strangely colored fur and skin. A human sat watching something on another tablet. He had several pieces of metal through his ears and lips and on his forehead. He looked up and stood when he saw Rick. The realistic dog tail between his legs started wagging. They hugged and smiled.

"SweetChops666," Rick said, "meet Anna!" He gestured for her to step up. She did so. Very reluctantly.

"Come," SweetChops666 said. He took her through some curtains and made sure they were shut. A fake scent of dog hid his own body odor. Anna found it revolting. There was a machine in a corner, and there were shelves with all kinds of cans and bottles. "What can I do you for?" he asked with a smile. "Sorry, my manners. What are your pronouns?"

"What are pronouns?" she asked. There was an awkward pause.

"Never mind. Let's color you. What would you like?"

"Can you make me look like a red fox?" she asked, immediately thinking of Shawn.

"Easy," he replied, "let's get busy."

Anna had to roll down her overalls and remove her shirt. This made her very, very uncomfortable. She only did it because she had no other choice. The coloring itself was quick and painless. The spray made Anna's nose twitch, and the blue light made her eyes water.

He held a mirror so she could see herself. Anna was amazed. She still had white fluff on her chest and chin, but the rest of her body was auburn. Her paws and arms were black. She looked exactly like her friend!

"It suits you," said Rick when she came out. Rick tapped his paw on SweetChops666's tab. "It'll stay a day or two," SweetChops666 said, "just long enough to have a blast at the con."

"T-thanks," she said.

"I need some odor neutralizing spray as well," said Isidore. Rick showed them where to go.

Back in their room, Isidore dug into Anna's convention bag. He gave her the new human shirt. She took it out and held it up. On the back was the friendly springbok. "Afr—Afrif—2082—What does it say?" she asked, pointing at the letters.

"AfricaFur 2082, Super Platinum Sponsor," he said, then gave her a pair of shorts. They were black. Isidore took both pieces of clothes and sprayed them. Anna was stunned: she could not scent anyone or smell anything for a few moments. It felt like she'd gone blind! "You can put these on if you need to quickly hide your scent." They spent the rest of the day in their room, ordered room service again, and went to bed early.

Anna found Isidore in the small living area the next morning. He looked amused. "These people are total freaks," he said.

"What do you see?" she asked.

"Morning Anna. I'm just checking the itinerary. There are all sorts of *things* happening today," he said. "Panels and discussions on everything imaginable... and some things that are better not. There's an art auction. Writing workshops. Photoshoots. A parade..."

"Are we doing any of those things?" she asked.

"I'd prefer not, but—" she tilted her head, "Rick insisted we join him for a tour."

"Are we safe?" she asked.

"Maybe just as safe as being cornered in this tiny room," he said as he lifted his hands. Anna nodded.

Shawn sat with his back against a tree by the river, and Anna sat before him, between his legs. His muzzle was buried in her neck fluff. Their paws were folded on her lap. He could tell she was anxious. He wished he could make her feel better, but he could not. All he could do was to comfort her, while she was there. Hold her. He wanted to be with her all the time. He liked touching her. He liked her scent.

"You are such a good friend, Shawn," she said after a long silence. She raised her head and rubbed the side of his face with her muzzle. He squeezed her tight and felt a pleasant discomfort in his loins. He sighed, lowered his muzzle, and rested his chin on her shoulder again. He could feel her pulse and breathing quicken as he sniffed behind her ears, her neck and shoulders, and near her armpits, just above her tiny teats. They both knew the time was not right yet. But it would be very soon.

Decompilation moved up by two percent.

Drones had explored the outside of the hotel and conference center. There was only one place that looked promising. "Look here," Handler said, pointing at his tablet. FEL9 gave an uninterested look over his shoulder. "There's a service entrance—one floor up—inside the garbage room. Let's go check it out."

The smell was horrid. Both he and FEL9 wretched. There was a crash of bottles as another bag of trash fell down the chute and landed in a dumpster. A compacting machine flexed and crushed it, sending a swarm of flies scrambling for new garbage to eat. In the furthest, filthiest corner, they saw the scaffold and the doors. It was too high for Handler to reach. "Can you reach it?" he asked.

He had not even finished speaking when FEL9 leapt. He grabbed onto a steel railing and pulled himself onto it. He turned back, as if to ask Handler, *"What are you waiting for?"*

"You have got to be kidding!" said Handler. "I could never get up there!"

"Too bad. Find another way in."

Handler gritted his teeth. FEL9's powerful paws made quick work of the tiny padlock that held the doors. He disappeared into a broad, dark gangway.

"Can you hear me?" asked Handler.

"Yes," replied the leopard through his earpiece.

"Let me know what you see. And remember—we must try to catch that fox alive."

"I will try," said the leopard. He did not sound very convincing.

"I think the jackal suits you!" complemented Rick. "You really should think about making your first fursona a jackal!"

Isidore groaned. The jackal head was giving him a pain in the neck. It would have been unbearable, if it weren't for the built-in air conditioning. He kept Anna in his peripheral vision. Her tiny frame was barely visible through the soup of mammalæ, fursuiters, non-fursuiters, and confused tourists who had ended up there by accident.

The dealer's den and the crowd were much bigger than the day before. Rick knew many of the dealers by name. "Hey AngelM0le! How's business?"

"Doing well," said a scrawny female in a shaggy brown kimono. "Who's the jackal?"

"This is my friend, Isidore. But I call him Saint. And this is Anna, his fox companion."

"Oh wow, a real fox!" she said, "Pleased to meet you two. Can I offer you a sketch?"

"Of course you can!" said Rick before Isidore could speak. "They're still very new to the furry scene, but I can tell they are already warming to it. Let's give them a little souvenir of their first convention!"

Isidore groaned again. He had long deactivated the facial tracking feature to avoid embarrassing his friend. AngelM0le made them sit on a low bench before a green screen. She looked them over, took a picture with her tablet, and made some outlines. "Great! Check back with me tomorrow afternoon for the finished piece."

Handler sat at a small cafe near the conference center. He listened attentively, trying hard to picture what FEL9 was doing. For a while, all he heard was paw steps and lively conversation that came and went. "Ooh! Such a powerful kitty! Can we have a selfie?" someone asked. "Can I have a paw print?" someone else asked. Handler heard the leopard growl. The voices quickly went away. His hair stood on end.

"FEL9!" Handler scolded. "Stop drawing attention to yourself, you imbecile! Give them what they want. You need to blend in if you want to find that fox!"

"Fine," the big cat murmured.

"Where are you now?" Handler asked.

"On floor seven. I have not scented them yet."

"Keep sweeping those floors," instructed Handler. Remember to use the stairs. You can check the lifts later."

"You already told me that."

"Let me know if you smell anything. I'm still trying to figure out a way to get in." Handler patted the dart gun under his shirt. He was livid that he couldn't be there to control his mammal. He didn't trust FEL9 on his own. The waiter brought him another cup of coffee.

Isidore and Anna joined Rick for a hearty meal over lunchtime in the headless lounge—the only place fursuiters were allowed to remove their heads. Rick then took them to the art show, where there were some surprisingly good pieces for sale. There were also some other pieces that showed *highly unrealistic portrayals* of the mammalæ reproductive system. Neither he nor Anna found them appetizing.

They went back to their room in the late afternoon. Isidore sighed, took the handle, paused. Frowned. It felt... different. He looked back at Anna whose eyes showed terror.

"He was here," she whispered. He gave her a moment to properly take in the scent. He then gestured for her to follow him down the passage. "A large male feline," she whispered, "We are in danger!"

"It's not safe to go inside," whispered Isidore. "He might be waiting for us. I'll alert con security immediately."

They were escorted back to their room by three members of convention security. With pepper spray at the ready, they pushed the door in. Two entered and one waited outside. A few moments later, they emerged. "Come."

Anna sniffed. Even Isidore could now smell the big cat as they stepped inside. Their towels were on the floor. The minibar stood open. There were tear marks in their bedding. Isidore iced over when he saw his portable and the still running MæSIM upside down on the floor. The link cable between them was stretched to its absolute limit. The sim's power cord was a few centimeters away from being ripped from the wall.

"We have a dangerous mammal on the loose," said one of the security staff into his earpiece. "A large male leopard. Please inform all convention staff. Do not engage with this mammal but inform security immediately. Please request the assistance of mammal control."

Isidore hardly noticed what was happening around him. He had already placed his portable and the MæSIM on the kitchen table and was running various integrity checks. His sturdy portable seemed okay. The MæSIM, on the other hand, had a couple of corrupted megabytes on its internal storage. It was very concerning. Though it probably was nothing that the built-in error-correction code couldn't fix, Isidore was again reminded how fragile it was. How fragile *everything* was. *"If only I had mammal.img..."*

They remained in their room as a different convention security officer—a German Shepherd Dog—guarded the door on the outside. Nobody said a word. The only sound was that of his typing and Anna foraging through the mini-bar. There was not the usual rain of clicks; Isidore typed slowly. It was as if he were afraid of drawing attention to himself. Anna licked her chops. She was about to tear open another packet of mammal biscuits when the guard knocked softly and entered. He still had his paw to his ear. He nodded, then looked at them. "Okay," he said. "I will tell them." Anna's ears perked and Isidore looked up. "We have him."

Anna stuffed the packet of biscuits into her bag and slung it over her shoulders. Isidore stuck his head back into the jackal, and they left the room. The dog escorted them to the elevator, which had to be cleared of all other bodies. They went down to the second floor where they were greeted by the senior convention security officer, a human. They were led down the passage to a heavy door. It was unmarked. The senior officer tapped the back of his hand on the reader. It beeped. "Go inside."

From the outside, it looked like any unused space, but the inside was a lot more interesting. It was a repurposed conference room which served as the central command of convention security. Several security officers—most of them German Shepherd dogs—stood around, awaiting orders. There were several tables with monitors on them; their cables ran to a central computer cabinet in the middle of the carpeted floor. Volunteer staff— mostly human—monitored the various video feeds. Some of them had half-eaten parcels of food and cans of energy drink beside them. Others were resting, lounging before a television. They watched animated movies from the Furry Age of Resistance, the early twenty-first century. In the far back of the room were a couple of temporary cages. Most of them were empty, but one held a particularly sad-looking dog, sitting calmly with a muzzle over his maw. Another held a meerkat who was having conversations with himself. In the last one lay the leopard. "We've had to dart him," explained the mammalæ control officer in brown, "so we have not had a chance to interrogate him."

"We found him sneaking around—naked—in an off-limits part of the conference center. He became aggressive when we confronted him."

Isidore smiled. "The bastard was probably changing his clothes to make himself harder to spot. Good work guys. Are they going to take him away?"

Mammal control nodded. "We are going to finish the paperwork. When my colleagues arrive, we'll take him to the pound. He won't bother you again."

Anna frowned and stepped away from the group. She approached the cage carefully, as if not to wake the unconscious beast. They watched her as she gave him a good look-over, then stuck her snout through the bars and sniffed. Again. And again. She turned slowly back towards the humans. Her face wrought with fear. "It is not him."

An eerie silence fell on the room. Then there was a commotion. "CA1-, 2 and 3 move out!" said the commanding officer. "Sweep the place!"

"Yes sir!"

The mammal control officer was red in the face. He stuffed a new dart into his gun and followed. "High alert," the officer told the monitoring staff. "If you see something, say something!"

He turned to Isidore and Anna. "You can't stay here."

"But why?" cried Anna.

"If he gets in here, our surveillance systems could collapse," he explained. "You will endanger us all. You will have to go. CA4 will escort you back to your room."

"No!" cried Isidore. "We can't go all the way up there again. He could be waiting for us around any corner. We need to find somewhere close."

"Where then?"

"Hang on." Isidore whipped out his tablet, scrolled. His eyes tracked the moving text, and his lips moved silently. He pointed at his tablet. "Here."

CA4 unlocked the door for her and she stepped inside. It was a cozy space. She scented mammal bodies, smelled alcohol and fruit. There were colorful bags and small tables on the floor. Mammalæ sat around, drank, and sucked on little straws that made them blow smoke through their noses. Some were talking, and some others were looking at their tablets. They all seemed very relaxed. There wasn't a human in sight. The floor was made of fake wood and felt slippery beneath her paws. Large black boxes stood in every corner of the room. There were more in front of a large one that was covered with a thick black sail. A lemur stood behind a tall wooden table that was closed at the front. There was a fountain before him and many colorful bottles on a large shelf behind. He had a drink in his paw. The ceiling had long metal beams with all sorts of machines hanging from them.

Anna stood for a moment just staring. She had no idea where she was.

"Hello there!" greeted a golden labrador. He took a puff from his straw. "Take a seat young lady. Get yourself a drink."

Anna nodded, sat down between the dog and a friendly looking zebra. She took the bag of biscuits from her bag and stuffed a few into her maw. "Sorry," she said, "I have never been to a place like this."

"What is your name?" asked the dog.

"Anna," she said.

"That's a cute name!" He smiled. "My name is Woofles and my zebra friend here is called Safari." He took another drag from his straw. The smoke smelled of fruit.

"First convention, eh?" remarked Safari. "Well, as you've seen, it's a crazy place. Humans trying to be mammalæ. Wearing those ridiculous suits. And, as you know, us emotional support mammalæ who must tag along."

"Emotional support mammal?" asked Anna.

"Oh, you're not one?"

"Sorry," she said, "I do not know what that means. I am a research mammal."

"Let me explain," said Woofles. He cleared his throat. "Some humans—ones with lots of money—get themselves real-life mammalæ companions. Pets, if you'd like."

"They bring us to these conventions. Mostly to show off," remarked a meerkat with a glass of light blue liquid in his paw. "It gets overwhelming. So many people want to touch us. Take pictures with us... That's why we have our own little place. Humans are not allowed in here."

"They have their own lounges."

"Oh, yes," said Woofles. "Like the fursuiters. You've seen many of those, right? It is against their religion to be seen without their silly heads on. So, they have their own lounge where they can cool down and have a drink with other headless beasts. Crazy right?" He upturned his paws and rolled his eyes. "So, what's your story? What is your master like?"

"He is a good man," Anna said. "But we are fleeing from a leopard who wants to catch us!"

"Oh wow," said Woofles. "And," Anna said, "we know he is here!"

"Shit, that's scary!" said Safari. "Is there anything we can do to help?"

"Maybe—just—let me know if you scent or hear him?"

"Have a puff," said Woofles. "It will calm your mood."

"No thank you." Anna stuck her paw into the packet and devoured the rest of the biscuits.

Safari looked up and flicked his ears. There was a beep, but the door did not open. There was a bump. And another. By now the conversation in the room had died down, and everyone's eyes were on the door.

Anna leapt up. "He's here!" she whispered with her paws outstretched and hackles raised.

"Quick! Hide!" whispered Safari. "There!"

More bumps followed. They grew louder and more powerful. A pause. Then a mighty crash as the door tore from its lock. The mammalæ collectively gasped and gawked as the scary apex predator stepped inside. The room was silent as the grave. The barman dropped his drink on the floor. The leopard looked around and sniffed deeply.

"She is here," he growled. "I want the fox. I want her now!"

"She left," said Safari, bravely fighting his instinct to run. "She was only here for a while. Said she needed to go to one of those panels." There was a murmur. Unimpressed, the leopard walked up to him, grabbed him by the collar of his shirt and lifted him from his seat. He pressed him against the nearest wall and bared his fangs. Safari gasped for his breath and grabbed at the predator's paws. His hooves swung helplessly beneath him. The other mammalæ scrambled. None of them had ever seen an aggressive mammal before. Some cowered behind their poofs. Others flattened themselves against the walls.

"Her scent is strong," the leopard said. "You are lying! Give her to me or I will rip out your throat!" Safari was too panicked to even speak. He quivered and his lips trembled. The big cat growled and dropped him to the floor. He scurried away. "Pathetic creature." The leopard breathed through his nose and looked around the room again. He scented her, but he didn't see her. He walked to the bar and looked behind it. He growled low when he saw nothing there but a petrified lemur. He checked the ceiling. He checked behind the speakers. Nothing. There was only one other place now she could be. The muscles on his back rolled and he popped his neck as he slowly approached the DJ's station. His posture was feral and threatening. He wasn't walking—he was stalking. There was no sound other than his paw steps.

He stopped just a few feet away, flexing his claws. "Come out fox!"

When there was no answer, he arched his back. He leapt over the station and landed crouching on the other side. Only his ears and the tip of his tail stuck out. "What—?!"

His torso emerged slowly. There was a deep frown on his spotted face. In his claws, a cotton sack. He sniffed it. Ripped it to shreds with his powerful claws. Strips of grey overalls and white cotton fell out. He gathered these, held them to his nose and sniffed. He gave a blood-curdling growl. She had tricked him!

"We... told you," said Safari, now a lot less cocky than before. The leopard showed his fangs to him as he stormed out the door. There were a few moments of perfect silence. "He's gone," someone whispered. "You can come out now, Anna."

The DJ's station shifted slightly. The black sail at the back opened. The vixen squirmed out from the tiny space between the underside of the turntables and the top of the equipment in the cabinet below. She wore a convention t-shirt and black shorts. She gasped for air. "Thank you," she heaved. "Thank you. Everyone!" She held her paws together before her face. There was a round of applause. "Here, here for Anna!"

She left. The mammalæ then all moved to form a long line by the bar.

Isidore walked beside CA4. The dog was alert. His whiskers twitched, and his keen eyes scanned the passage before them. His ears perked up as they stopped by a stairwell. He sniffed deeply and gestured for Isidore to step aside. He carefully removed the pepper spray from his belt. Reached out to open the door. But before he could, it swung open violently, smacking him on the side of his muzzle. He yelped. Isidore turned around and bolted as FEL9 and the dog engaged. The passage smelled of pepper. Looking back over his shoulder, Isidore saw FEL9 throw CA4 against the wall. The dog yelped again, collapsed, and did not get up.

The leopard turned towards Isidore, and Isidore ran. Around a corner, he nearly fell over Anna. "Anna! Run!" he barked. "Room 3a on the second floor! Go!" The vixen flung around and bolted as well.

FEL9 gained on Isidore with every step he took. He knew he had to do something. Fast. In a moment of courage—or stupidity—he swung around and blocked off the passage with his outstretched arms and parted legs. The big cat raised its claw to strike.

Time stopped.

There was a moment of absolute clarity. Isidore realized the jackal suit betrayed his true form. FEL9 could not harm *humans*. Not a moment too soon. He plucked off the jackal head and threw it at the leopard. FEL9 slashed, ripping the head to shreds, but stopped dead in his tracks. Isidore raised his hand and pointed his finger at the leopard's face. "Touch me and you will regret the day you were manufactured, you piece of feline shit!" The big cat stood less than a meter before him. He opened his giant maw and let out a roar that shook the floor. The man could smell his rotten breath. He could count its razor teeth. It felt like his intestines had all liquified. He nearly blacked out with fear. FEL9 didn't lower his claw. His eyes were honed on the human's throat. "I can kill you. With a single. Swipe. Of. My. Claw. You have nothing, you pathetic little plaything! Step aside. Now!"

"Your programming says you—won't harm—a human." Isidore spoke in a voice that sounded more like the squeak of a mouse than that of a man. He shook. The leopard looked like he was ready to pop an artery in his brain from anger. His face was drawn with rage. Isidore was right: his programming wouldn't allow him to hurt a human. He could not. He felt like making a snide remark, but he found he was unable to speak. Without turning away, without lowering his arms or closing his legs, he tip-toed backwards, away from the leopard. FEL9 followed him, moving closer with every step.

After about five steps, Isidore's survival instincts got the better of him. He turned and ran for all that he was worth, down the passage, closely pursued by the predator who was keeping up, hardly breaking a sweat. His heart pounded and his throat burned. The leopard could not harm him, but he could follow him. And he had no choice but to go to Anna. He could only hope his plan would work.

Seizing the opportunity, he ducked into a crowded elevator that had just opened its doors. He wormed his way right to the back, inviting angry looks from the other patrons, who were mostly human. They gasped when they saw he wasn't wearing his head. FEL9 tried to step into the confined space as well, but the buzzer immediately sounded. "Hey, you!" said a patron. You will have to wait for the next one. This one is full!"

The plaque before room 3a read *"The care and keeping of veteran and active-service mammalæ."* Isidore burst in. Anna was already there. She crouched in a tiny ball in the farthest corner of the room. She sat quivering. The room was quiet. Isidore ploughed through the audience, knocking over chairs. Cans of energy drinks spilled out on the carpet.

"Help!" he cried. There was a scuffle in the already jittery audience. Heavy paw steps neared. The door flung open again, and the snarling leopard burst inside. Unfortunately for him, he had come to the wrong place: some of the mammalæ in the audience were bodyguards. Some were sniffer dogs. Some were paramedic assistants. Security personnel. Firefighters. Cheetahs. Honey Badgers. Porcupines. Large muscular dogs. The bodyguards immediately leapt to protect their masters. Others, guided by years of training and instinct, leapt from their seats and pounced on the leopard. They knocked over chairs and the pedestal with the presenter's projector on it. FEL9 was strong and fast, but an eleven-strong pack of lesser- but still large-framed mammalæ had no problem taking him down.

He roared and swiped at their faces with his claw. A caracal rammed her claws into his arm. She hissed. A cheetah perched on his chest. A hyena had his paws around the leopard's neck. A mastiff held down the leopard's claws. He growled fearlessly in the big cat's face. The presenter went completely pale. The chaos had hardly settled when a handful of convention security, a duo of mammalæ control, and two police officers burst in.

"Freeze!" barked one of the police officers. In addition to several tasers, two handguns were now pointed at the leopard. Several dozen eyes looked up at them. The only sound now was a low, anguished growl and an uncomfortable shifting of seats. "Oh."

Seeing that the situation was under control, the officers lowered their firearms ever so slightly. "Keep calm. We got this."

Anna was in tears. She shook where she lay on the floor now. Isidore saw stars before his eyes. The mob that had taken the big cat down slowly pulled away, freeing the leopard to move again. "Easy big guy. No sudden moves, okay? We got permission to kill!" FEL9 rose slowly, his right paw and left cheek bled. He reluctantly raised his paws.

Handler stood at a distance. He watched in horror as mammalæ control and two police officers escorted FEL9 from the door. His paws were cuffed together. He was muzzled and there was an electro-shock collar-pole around his neck. Blue and green lights reflected off every glass surface, the many parked vehicles, and the faces of the curious onlookers. Convention staff tried to shoo away bloggers and streamers who clamored to get pictures or video. Mammalæ control shoved the leopard into the waiting van and shut the heavy steel door behind him. Handler plucked the communications device from his ear. He threw it in the ground and crushed it with his shoe.

Medical staff had given Isidore an injection to calm him down. The resident veterinarian did the same for Anna. There were now two mammalæ control officers stationed outside their room. Mildly sedated, Isidore sat quietly in the living area. It felt surreal. Rick was in the lobby, talking to the various bloggers and the media.

"They are gone for now," Isidore said in a defeated voice. "They will come back. And FEL9 will be angry."

"He is—the scariest thing I ever saw," said Anna. Her voice trembled.

"Yes," replied Isidore. "He is. But let me tell you something." Anna raised her head. "They sent the wrong mammal. They tried to scare us." Anna nodded slowly in agreement. "He is too big. Too strong. Too violent to be out in public. And," Isidore added, "he is very, very stupid." Isidore took a deep breath. "Do you want to visit Shawn?"

Anna nodded.

The drugs that Anna brought along from the real world excited and soothed her.

She was ready. She knew that he was ready, too. Their tails swished wildly as they took in each other's spicy scents. Her arms were draped around his neck, and his paws rested on her hips. His touch excited her. Their bellies rubbed together. Anna's heart raced. She smelled his breath and scented the musk of his coat. He scented her heat. It was intoxicating. Anna's breathing was shallow and fast. She raised her head, pushed out her chest and offered him her neck. He burrowed his nose deep into her fur and sniffed deeply. She closed her eyes, parted her lips and raised her muzzle. She waited for him to kiss her. And he did so. Passionately.

The worst of the tranquilizers had worn off, but Isidore still struggled to keep his eyes open. He had already finished two cans of Blast. He nearly fell asleep at his portable when something caught his eye. He was suddenly wide awake. The console displayed an unfamiliar stream of data, and the decompilation progress rose fast. His heart raced as he examined the end of the log. Shawn and Anna had mated. They were having sex. Her legs moved rhythmically. She made the tiniest *yip! yip! yip!* sounds where she lay. Isidore gave a cry of joy and threw his hands into the air. For a few moments, there was a stormy exchange of data, which he captured. His screen scrolled with hundreds upon hundreds of lines of mammalæ code.

But his joy was short-lived. The progress indicator did rise by a whole fourteen percent, but the code was still incomplete. It now stood at ninety-six percent. His mouth was suddenly dry.

"This—this cannot be!" Isidore said aloud and pushed his hands through his imaginary hair. His hands trembled. For the two foxes to mate was not enough. It was never enough! The puzzle was still incomplete. He had checked and double-checked the specifications. He had exercised every possible thought, emotion, and combination thereof, two times over. But there was still a piece missing. It was a terrible turn of events.

Shawn held Anna tight where she lay with her head on his fluffy chest. His paws gently stroked her behind her ears, and her paws were on his thighs. Their scents had mixed. His body had become one with hers. She was still wet. In a few precious moments, they created something new. Something magical. The rustic river bubbled before them, and there were crickets chirping in the woods. It was perfect. Yet Anna seemed sad and scared. "Did—did we do the right thing, Shawn?" she asked in a tiny voice.

Shawn didn't understand. "What do you mean, dear Swiftpaw?"

"We are mated," she said. "But... you are in the forest. And I am in a different place. How will we be together?" She paused. "When I have our kits, will they live here? Or will they be with me? Will you ever see them?"

Shawn was shocked. "I... don't know my love," he said. "I never thought of that! I hardly thought at all! I scented your heat—and I knew I had to start a family with you. Immediately."

"It was so special when you took me," she said. A tear rolled over her cheek. She sniffed. "Every time—I go—I am scared I will not see you again."

Shawn squeezed her tight. "Me too, Swiftpaw. Me too."

They sat in silence.

Isidore brought Anna back, but only when he had stopped crying himself.

ESCAPE

There was a buzz and a clack. The heavy steel door swung open. Handler, escorted by two guards, stepped inside. He looked around. There were eight cells on each side of the long passage. They were separated by concrete dividers, and there were thick, steel bars in the front. The floor was covered in worn, sticky black tiles. There were only one or two light fixtures on the ceiling. The place smelled like a zoo.

In the first cell was an intoxicated Doberman Pinscher who hung from the bars and mumbled to himself. Two cages down was a rabid skunk in a strait jacket. He foamed at the mouth and aggressively smacked his head against the bars. FEL9's cage was towards the end.

"Can you give us a few minutes?" Handler asked. The guards nodded. "We'll be right outside if you need us. Just shout."

FEL9 looked up from where he sat on the floor in the corner of his cell. He stood up and went to the bars. Handler did not greet him and kept a safe distance.

"FEL9," he started as he shook his head, "How pathetic." The leopard's jaw was tensed up and his eyes narrowed. His ears were flat against his head. "Capture a little fox. Bring her to me. How the *fuck* did you manage to screw this up so bad? Look at you! In the fucking pound! With a muzzle over your fat, fucking face!"

"I... am sorry, master."

"You better be fucking sorry, moron. You've made us look like total imbeciles! SFA are not impressed. You are designed to win wars, for fuck's sake. You were one bit flag short of turning that man into hot porridge. But you let both him and that fox slip away." Handler took a breath. "HQ is scrambling to get the paperwork for your release. It's a tough sell. Aggressive behavior in a civilian setting is the kind of thing that gets your kind an early retirement."

FEL9's lip twitched. He showed the side of a fang.

Handler cooled. "Anyway, you are not coming out tonight. Think about what happened today. And what I said. Make sure it doesn't happen again!"

"Yes... master." FEL9 turned and sat down to sulk in the corner of his cage.

Isidore sat in bed with his portable on his lap. Anna stared at the television. It spoke low, but not soft. It showed cities on fire. Stripes of light in the sky. Entire coastlines swept away by waves as tall as mountains. Chaos and death.

It hardly registered. Isidore knew all that mattered to her was that she had to leave her mate alone in the woods. In their last spoken words, she promised to return. He knew it would not happen.

He tried to put those thoughts out of his mind. He needed to focus. "There's something I need to do," he said.

Anna looked up slowly. The expression on her face was blank.

He paused for a moment, then pressed a key. There was a sort of cascading sound. "Ok, Anna, listen. This is very important. When we step out of those doors, absolutely anything could happen. I've transferred a substantial amount of money to your chip. If we get separated, it will keep you going for at least a couple of weeks. It will help you travel. Buy food. But use it sparingly, as it will run out. And every time you tap, they may be able to track you." He pressed some more keys. "I've done what I can to hide your identity, but it's messy. I've made your master some gal who's fighting abroad in the US. I've removed all travel restrictions from your profile."

Anna nodded.

"Unfortunately, I can't hack into the police's database, so they might still look for *someone* like you—if SFA decide to go to the police." Anna's face was still expressionless. She nodded and turned back to the television. Isidore put the portable on his bedside table and took his tablet. He made a call. "I can't thank you enough, buddy," he told Rick. "You saved our lives. Sorry about the mess."

"It's okay," replied the green and white fox. "You didn't trash the place. Completely. But I was worried for a few moments there. Only the security staff know what really happened."

"I don't know when we'll be able to make contact again."

"I understand Saint. I wish you the best of luck. Oh, and can I say goodbye to Anna?"

Isidore nodded. Anna's ears perked up. She got up slowly and took the tablet from him.

Rick smiled at her. "It was an absolute pleasure having you as one of our guests."

She tried to smile. Isidore took his tablet again and ended the call. He pulled his freshly laundered shirt over his head. Anna slipped on the new overalls that Isidore had organized. He stuffed his machines into his rolling suitcase and closed the lid. He kept his tab in his pocket. "We can't risk going back to Cath. We can't go back to my place. We can't stay here—there's only one place of safety we can still go to. Far away."

"I'm going to help you on your way, Anna. Then, I'm going to hand myself over. I'll try to stall them as much as I can. That will be your best chance to get away." Isidore explained to her that they were supposed to leave the next day, but they snuck out of the hotel just before midnight. An Autotaxi waited for them by the grand entrance. Isidore nervously tapped in.

"Where would you like to go?" asked the bodiless voice.

"Take us to the station."

The journey was short—the station was only a few blocks away. *"Thank you for traveling with us,"* the taxi said. Isidore had already opened the door to get out when Anna pulled him back by the sleeve.

"Am—am I going to see Shawn again?" she spoke in a tiny voice.

Isidore bowed his head and closed his eyes. "Probably not."

Anna's ears flattened to her head. Her shoulders dropped and she wiped an eye with her paw. "Are you sure there is no way? I just want to see him one more time. To say goodbye."

Isidore was anxious. "Every minute we delay is a minute more they have to find us. And if they find us, you won't see Shawn anyway." He could see she was conflicted. She looked up at him with sad, scared eyes.

"I want to see him again. Even if I die."

Isidore hesitated. Then closed the door. "Taxi," he said, "please take us to the foreshore container yard."

As they rounded the last traffic circle, just past the docks, the taxi suddenly slowed down. It pulled onto the side of the road, and its hazard lights started blinking. Isidore's tablet vibrated. The taxi's invisible voice spoke. *"Mister Robert Fisk, we have just been notified of a criminal investigation opened against you. To protect our organization from potential criminal liability, this journey has been terminated effective immediately. You may disembark or, alternatively, you may request this vehicle to take you to the nearest police station. Free of charge."*

"We'll disembark," he said.

"We would like to thank you for traveling with us."

The air outside was thick with moisture, and it smelled like rain. The taxi drove off into the night. He and Anna stood on the side of a misty road in the glow of a lone streetlight. He looked at her. She looked at him. He dug into his pocket and removed a tiny flashlight. He switched it on and tightened his grip around the handle of the carry case. "Anna," he said, "How fast can you run?"

Anna was much faster than him. She took the carrying case from him when she saw he could not keep up. They climbed over a fence. On the other side, Isidore stopped. His hands were on his knees. He breathed heavily and sweat streamed down the side of his face. When he managed to catch his breath, he started pointing his light. He was looking for something. When he did not see it, he braced to run again but fell. Anna helped him to his feet.

They moved slower now. There were rows and rows of containers. He shined his light against them and the yellow letters painted on the ground. At last, he found what he was looking for. It was a small container, red in color. There were Russian letters on the side. Isidore pulled a key from his pocket and unlocked the door. It opened with a squeal. When the light fell on the inside, Anna recoiled in horror. She recognized the insides and the smell of the place. It was the worst thing imaginable. There was a silent machine in the corner that made no light. On the floor was a cage. It was where she lay tied up with her tiny body stuck full of pipes and wires. Empty bags hung from the ceiling. There were wires. Pads. There were syringes, gloves and bottles. Bandages and restraints. The entire place stank of pee and feces. Hers. Anna suddenly remembered that she was trapped in there for weeks, without being able to move. Or scream. It was a fox-sized torture chamber built especially for her. Anna wet herself. She spun around to run. Isidore grabbed her overalls by the strap. Adrenaline made her incredibly strong. "Wait—Anna!"

"I am not going there!" Anna yipped as she tried to break from his grip. She did not even want to turn her face back towards the doors. "Anna, listen," Isidore pleaded with panic in his voice. "I—can only imagine—"

"You—will—never!" she yipped. She snarled. When he still held on, she turned back and bit his hand. He opened his fist in fright. She darted off into the night.

Isidore's lungs heaved. He went down on his knees and placed his bleeding hand on his head. He struggled to catch his breath. A few minutes later, after he managed to compose himself, he stood inside the container, a handful of tiny lights glowing back at him. He had restarted the container's power supply. The batteries were low, but they would give him enough time to shred his portable. And the MæSIM. The glow of his monitor cast blurry shadows on the inside of the dreadful place. He brought the simulator out of hibernation and was immediately greeted by several amber lights at the front. It did not look good. On the console, on his portable, he saw the system run the diagnostics process. There were several hundred megabytes of corrupted data now. "Isidore?" At first, he thought he was imagining things and ignored the voice. "Isidore? Master?" It was Anna. His heart skipped a beat. He turned away from his monitor and saw her trembling just outside the open door. Her legs were squeezed together, and her tail was between her legs. "Anna. Why did you come back?"

"I wanted to say goodbye to Shawn. But," she pointed, "I am scared of that place."

His heart ached for her. "You won't be alone this time. I'll be here with you. I will hold your paw." The MæSIM had finished performing its checks. Anna lay down on her side, on the tiny, soiled mattress in the middle of the container's cold, steel floor. He kneeled beside her and stroked her head and ears gently. He could feel her tremble. He issued the necessary commands and plugged her in. He waited until she was immersed until he closed the container doors and bolted them from the inside. He examined the console on his portable. The MæSIM still produced valid data, which was a small relief. But for how long? He bit his tongue before he could say, "Be careful, Anna."

Anna stood in the middle of the clearing and was immediately filled with dread. She sniffed and looked around her. The forest was different now. There were no scents or smells. The sky was solid grey. The trees had no leaves. Everything was silent. There was no running water and the wind didn't move. Everything seemed... dead? A few steps ahead of her, she saw Shawn. He sat staring into the woods. His back was hunched. His ears were against his head.

"Shawn?" His ears perked up ever so slightly as he looked over his shoulder.

"Swiftpþw." He slowly pushed himself off the ground and turned to her. There was sadness on his face. He looked... strange. The fur on his body and his tail was not fluffy. It seemed clumped and rough.

She ran to him and they embraced. Anna lay her muzzle on his shoulder. His scent was just a whisper, and his fur felt cold and lifeless in her paws. "What is happening?!"

"I feel so drain*êd," he said. "It feels like I am jüst wasting away. Falling apaˆrt."

Anna pulled back. His voice sounded horrible. "Your voice!" she cried looking him in the eyes. "What is happening to your voice?"

"It is gettÐÌng worse," he said.

"Come!" agonised Anna, tugging at his paw. "Let's get out of here!"

Shawn looked down and shook his head. "I can't lŒve this place. You must get Ì‹ out. I don't know what h...Àt7Pèappens when it comes apart. Ìì don't want ¥ou to g˜ÇE%t hurt."

The ground below her feet changed while they spoke. It was solid green now. There was no grass, and the trees had lost their branches. They were solid brown pillars. "I will not leave you!" she cried, grabbing and pulling his arm.

Shawn turned to run, ready to shake her paw from him, but he paused. "I Mǒd%ost go, Anna. This can't be stÒ%opped. I don't w]Ø‹Ëant you to see Y9uä me die. But—" he paused. "Here is søhmething to rem‹Ember me by." He turned back towards her and touched her cheek. His paws were solid blocks now. All the softness was gone. He caressed the back of her head and pressed his cold, hard lips against hers. She closed her eyes. Her body stiffened as he kissed her, but it was more than a kiss. It was not like anything she had ever felt before. It was a rush of warmth that flowed through her. A bright light filled her closed eyes.

When their lips parted, Anna fell forward, right through him. He was no longer solid. Everything except his face was now squares and triangles. Strange colors filled the gaps between them. He looked at his paws in horror. He backed away from her. He ran. Shawn's movements were now choppy.

Anna reached out towards him and shouted his name. "It's no ò^ƒ)L use," he said. She could hardly hear what he said. "I am mmm not ²™öj[eu€¾ long for this pla+ÆjãZ+Ö‰ ce. Good by yyy yyy SwifÝæ'Õ"£—Q. I lov*ê you."

"Shawn—I love you too!" His face was now a blocky mess as well. It could not show emotion, but Anna was sure he looked back at her one last time. His arm did something to his head that was now a bright green block with white stripes. He stood. Frozen. Neither his arms, legs or tail made any movement, even though he still moved away from her. His head and body disappeared, leaving only his arms and legs. He then disappeared completely.

```
Unhandled exception at 0x9283 F1AA 42CD 1901
in mammal.runtime:

Unexpected end of stream. Attempt to auto-
recover in 600 seconds…
```

The MæSIM's lights flickered. Amber turned red. It still pinged, but the terminal had stopped scrolling. *"I guess that's the end of Shawn,"* thought Isidore. It was all for naught. He switched tabs and issued the eject command for Anna. The console informed him that some processes were still ongoing and that he needed to wait before removing the plug.

The trees had all disappeared. The only thing that was still there was a solid, flat surface on which she stood. Around on all sides was solid black.

"Get me out of here!" she yipped. Nothing happened. She felt a prickly sensation along her spine. She took a deep breath. Raised her head and outstretched her paws to touch the sky above. She felt a powerful tug and an incredible rush. It filled every part of her body. Every strand of her fur stood upright. There was a moment of perfection. Nothingness. She was no longer in that awful place.

Isidore waited anxiously for the unspecified processes to finish. He paced up and down between his portable and Anna's still frame on the floor. Something wasn't right. He needed to get her out. They were losing power, and the simulator was careening towards a crash. He turned back towards his portable and frowned.

He had failed to notice the progress indicator had hit one hundred percent. The key generation process had already started. He blinked in disbelief. *"How...?"* He examined the console. The last new code—four percent in total—came from Shawn, not Anna. *"How could it be?"* he wondered as he blinked and looked a second time. He looked at the time. He couldn't be sure if the event occurred before or after the MæSIM threw the first exception. Scrolling up, he saw a transmission unlike he had ever seen before. It was completely void of external input or internal processes. Its signature did not match any known emotion or thought. The content was a garbled mess. For all intents and purposes, it was white noise. Yet, it was not. The checksum passed just fine. The hairs on his neck stood on end.

"I think..." he said aloud, "I might have just decompiled the mammal soul."

mammal.img was now complete. His hands trembled as he kicked off the scripts he had prepared. Most passed. Only a handful completed with warnings. It was the most powerful moment of his existence. He had another shock as he turned around: Anna sat up, her eyes wide open, with the linkup cable still attached to her head. She was very much alive, but her eyes were empty and dead. "He is gone," she said. Her extremities jolted slightly as she reached back and clumsily unplugged herself.

Isidore gaped. "How did you do that?"

"Do what?"

"How did you come back from the forest on your own?"

"I do not know," she said in a trembling voice. She was bewildered for a few moments. Then she broke down. The MæSIM's fans stopped, and all its lights went out. Isidore kneeled beside her, placed his hand on the back of her head, and gently stroked her behind the ears. The wailing sounds from her lips weren't that of a mammal. They were the sounds of an injured, little creature in the wild. It was dreadful. In the background, the beeping had grown regular and desperate until finally there was a clack. The container fell into blackness and the air stopped circulating. The space grew moist and stale as the temperature rose slowly. The wailing turned to sobbing. The sobbing became deathly silence.

"We are going to have to open those doors," said a human voice from the dark. "But before we do, I just want to say something. I never meant for things to end this way. I am sorry, Anna. I couldn't have asked for a more loyal and devoted companion. And such a great helper. You deserved better than this. I wish I could give back all I ever took from you." The first rain drops fell on the container shell.

"Yes," said a tiny vixen voice after a long spell of silence. "I wanted a different life. But I forgive you. I know you cared. In the end." There was another long pause. "Can I have your light?"

Isidore sat with his head in his palms as Anna dug through the debris on the floor. She treaded carefully to avoid the syringes and shattered glass. Right at the back of the container, she found what she was looking for: her old backpack. There was a loud knock from the outside of the container. It sounded hollow, like a batten. "This is the police! Step out with your hands above your heads!"

"It was only a matter of time now," agonized Isidore. "We need to open those doors. Anna," he said. "Run. Run. Run as fast as you have ever run before! Get away from these people. Get away from this place! Use the funds I gave you to get away from this city. You are too precious for them to kill. As long as you can run, you are safe." He could not see her nodding in the dark. "Ready? Three. Two. One." Isidore flung the doors open with force, drew their attention to himself with the flashlight in his hand. He dove to cover Anna's escape. She slipped behind his back and between the legs of two officers who stood them down. High-voltage darts that were meant for her sunk into his skin. He curled in on himself and convulsed as he fell and lay shaking on the concrete. "Get her!" someone shouted.

Anna ran. It rained. The yellow lights were dim, but she could see a few paces ahead. Freedom was within her grasp. There were paw steps behind her. She hardly had a chance to look. A powerful claw ripped the back of her overalls and pinned her to the ground. Her overalls protected her knees, but her elbows were scuffed. She squirmed to get up, but she stood no chance.

"Hello fox," FEL9 growled. "Trying to make a run for it? Again?" He did not give her time to answer. "They asked me to try and capture you alive," he said. "They said *try*. I'm tired of trying. Prepare to die!" He rolled her onto her back, as if she was a ragdoll. He leaned on her chest with his paw, squeezing all the air from her. He opened his giant maw and readied to close it around her neck. Anna saw her life flash before her eyes. Her mind shut down. There was a bone-chilling slop sound. Blood streamed from FEL9's mouth and onto Anna's chest—

—where she plunged her hunting knife through the soft skin under the leopard's chin. He roared, more from shock than pain. Momentarily, he raised his paw from her chest. She gasped. FEL9 swung his claw. They tore a chunk of fur from Anna's shoulder, but her airborne blade found his collar and peeled skin from bone. A bloody roar left his lips again as he stepped back, then leapt forward, closing his claws around Anna's neck.

Her paws were always swift. The cuts she made to her prey were clean and precise. Now foaming from the mouth, all of that was gone. Anna rammed the blade into the leopard's eyes, neck and abdomen. His arms. The side of his chest. His lungs. His heart. Violently. Again, and again. Blood spattered from every cut and sprayed from his torso. Her overalls were soaked in blood. It was all over her face and arms. It was inside her mouth and nose. She tasted it. It spilled onto the concrete.

His dead weight fell on her. She felt him squirm. Anna managed to push his body off her. She pushed herself up to run but stopped. She turned back for a moment. The leopard's frame had crumpled. His arms and legs would not push him off the ground. With his throat slashed he could no longer speak, but his terrified eyes spoke a haunting final phrase. *"This was not a fair fight."* FEL9 lay down his head. What little blood was left continued to seep out in the rain.

Anna darted off into the night, clinging onto her hard-won freedom. And her bloodied knife.

Water sifted down and a cold wind howled. Anna's overalls and coat were a soaking mess. There was blood on her clothes. There was blood on her paws. There was blood hardening on the blade of her knife. She was not tired or hungry. Her heart still pounded, and her breathing was rushed. *"They are looking for me,"* she thought. *"They will find me at any moment!"* She still ran for all her worth. Anna climbed over a tall fence at the edge of the depot and landed ankle-deep in muddy water. She paused and looked. There was pale light from the streetlights of the road high above. There were railway tracks before her. Anna ducked between gutted carriages, rusting railway equipment, and uneven tracks. Her eyes struggled. They darted side to side. She finally found what she was looking for: an open door.

Anna jumped into a rusty passenger car. The steel floor was wet and cold beneath her paws, and rain fell through holes in the rusted ceiling. It smelled of rust—and alcohol? There were burned-out seats along the middle aisle, and there was trash in the overhead storage. Dark lights hung by wires from the roof. The doors of the carriage were ripped off. Many of the windows were smashed in. It wasn't a welcoming place, but if she was lucky, they wouldn't find her there. It took her a while to calm down. She was about to sit on the remains of a rear-facing seat, when there was movement further along the carriage. She leapt from her seat. In the darkness lay a man. His body was on the floor between the last two seats. He wore ragged old clothes. His mouth was half-open. In his hand was an empty bottle. She sniffed. It was where the smell of alcohol came from.

"You are, one of thothe animal-peopleth," he slurred. Anna arched her back and snarled at him. Canines out and hackles raised. "Don hurth me," the man pleaded raising his free hand, "I just poorth drunke man!" Anna relaxed her shoulders. Slightly. From the way he scented, she knew he probably could not harm her. He didn't speak again.

Anna took off her clothes and wrung them out. She soaked them in water from outside. She managed to get most of the blood out. Anna then showered in the rain. The artificial coloring on her fur stained her hands. The auburn reminded her of

Shawn. Her heart felt sore. Anna hung her clothes over a seatback and sat down on the one across. The man snored loudly. For a long time, Anna sat quietly staring out one of the windows that was still intact. At the far end of the railyard, she saw the lights of a Metrorail move through a gap between two other gutted carriages.

The place made her even more sad. It was where things that were no longer useful came to die and fade away. *"Why am I here?"* she wondered. She thought about the things she saw. About the things that had happened. *"Where will I go?"* she wondered again, and *"Is it safe to sleep?"*

[####################] 100%

Freedom

The rain had stopped overnight. Anna woke up with the morning sun on her face. They had not found her. She was still free. Only an empty bottle remained of the man. He was gone—and so was her shirt and knife. Anna gritted her teeth. She peeked outside the door before stepping back onto the soggy soil. There were puddles of water everywhere. The tracks on the other side of the yard shone in the sun. She carefully made her way there. Anna climbed over a fence and landed on the side of a roadway. She turned right towards the city.

The sun was hot and bright now. Humans and mammalæ moved along the sidewalks. Motorcars slid by, and the smell of food was strong. Everything felt so normal. Anna looked around, scared. She wondered where to go.

"Good morning!" said a friendly voice beside her. Her heart nearly stopped. *"Welcome to the Mother City!"* it said, only just in time before she could run away. *"How may I be of assistance?"* It was a large, upright panel by the roadside. There was an image of a speaking woman in colorful clothing on it. She had dark skin, like some of the women Anna had seen in the city. She was friendly looking, but she had no scent.

"I need clothes," said Anna, folding her arms.

"No problem, miss!" said the friendly woman. *"There is a mammalæ shop not too far from here. Keep going straight. Turn left into Heerengracht Street. Continue past the circle, turn right into Van*

Riebeeck. *Is there anything else I can help you with?*" the woman asked.

"I want to buy a knife."

"*I am sorry,*" said the woman, "*carrying a knife in public is prohibited. You may order one online and it will be delivered to your registered home, or business address. Is there anything else I can help you with?*"

"I need to get away from the city."

"*We hate to see you go,*" she said. "*Did you at least enjoy your time with us?*"

"No."

"*Ok, never mind. Do you have any idea where you would want to go?*"

"As far away as I can."

"*If you are planning to go far, quickly, you might want to take the tube. The last and only stop is Johannesburg. We can, however, confirm that the first available departure with seats available only leaves in three days' time. If you want to get going quicker—or travel to a different city in between—it would be better to take the normal long-distance train. The farthest you can go in one unbroken journey, departing today, is Tshwane. The price for a second-class, one-way ticket is approximately forty thousand nine hundred and fifty-six Rand. You can buy the tickets at the station. Will that be all?*"

Anna nodded. "T-thanks."

She felt better when she put on her fresh new clothes in an alley. She dropped her old ones in a trashcan by the side of the road. Anna recognized the station, and her chest felt tight. A building and two roads between her and... freedom?

"Excuse me miss," said a voice from behind. Anna's body tensed. She was ready to run again, but she managed to control herself. Two mammal control officers stood on the wide walk beside her. One of them gestured for her to come closer. "Routine stop, miss. Would you mind showing us your paw?" Anna extended her paw half-way towards them, then paused. Her heart rumbled and she felt her empty tummy churn. The officer gestured impatiently with his scanner as his accomplice adjusted his belt. Anna swallowed as she extended her arm all the way. She closed her eyes. Beep. The man examined his display, tilted his head and looked at his colleague. They examined the display together.

"They are going to catch me!" thought Anna.

He looked at her again. "You may go, miss. Have a good day."

The station was busy. Many bodies moved around. There were large signs with arrows pointing in all different directions. There were pictures of trains, cars, and streetcars. There were shops. Food sellers. Humans and mammalæ with suitcases and carry bags. Anna's tail was drawn. She was overwhelmed and didn't know what to do! Her shoulders tensed. "You look lost dear," said an old nanny goat. "Can I help you?"

Anna turned towards her slowly. Nodded. "Please miss—I have never been on a far train before. What is a ticket? How do I get a ticket? What must I do?"

The goat smiled. "Don't worry dear. I'll help you." She gestured for Anna to follow her. She took her to a strange upright machine with a large glowing panel. She recognized some of the letters, but there were a lot of them. There were a couple of pictures and many colored lines as well. "Where are you going?"

"Tshwane."

"What class will you be traveling in?"

"What is a class?"

The nanny chuckled. "It means, do you want to sit in a carriage with many other people? Do you want to sit with fewer other people and get free food? Or do you want a small room for yourself?"

"I want a small room," said Anna. "I want to be alone."

The goat tapped the screen. "Good," she said, "all you have to do now is pay." She pointed at a small round pad.

Anna nodded. It was the only part that made any sense to her. She tapped the back of her paw. Beep.

"There you go young lady! Your ticket is now loaded to your tag. Tap your paw and go through those gates. Get on the train on platform five. Have a pleasant trip!"

Anna thanked her. She went through the gates and asked one of the station staff to show her where platform five was. "The train only leaves in an hour and five minutes," said a skunk in uniform. "What class are you traveling in?"

"I have my own room," she said.

"Oh, it's fine then," he said. "They usually let you guys on before the time. Travel well!"

After scanning her entry at the door, a friendly member of staff, a fennec, showed her to her cabin. It was near the end of a long, straight passage that smelled of flowers. The door slid open. Anna gaped.

It was like a tiny little house! It had a big window with curtains. A basin. A television. Two seats. The door closed behind her.

"*Hello miss,*" greeted the television, which now sprang to life with a colorful picture of a different city. "*Welcome to first class! I am at your service. Is there anything I can do for you? Snack and beverage service will start as soon as we depart.*" Anna stood in wonder for a moment, then took a seat. It was very comfortable. She looked up at the television but did not respond. She leaned back. Her eyelids felt heavy. "*You appear to be tired,*" the television said. "*Would you like me to make your bed?*" Anna nodded. "*Please stand up from the seats and I will do so.*" There was a whirr. Gently, the seats folded flat. In their place now was a comfy looking human bed. Anna didn't trust human beds: she was always scared of falling off. But she was too tired to care. She took off her clothes and lay down. She let out a tiny moan as she sunk away into the soft mattress and fresh-smelling linen. She curled up in a little ball, tucked her tail between her legs, and immediately fell asleep.

Anna walked beside Shawn. The soft white snow of her home came down from the white sky above. They held paws. Anna felt it in her tummy every time he looked at her. His scent was musky and wild. The smell around them was that of rotting wood and resting soil. His paws were warm, and he held hers gently. Their kits ran ahead of them, two little foxes with coats like snow, and one little vixen that was auburn like her mate. They laughed and shouted as they played. They ran ahead, then waited for their parents to catch up. They threw balls of snow at one another. Anna and Shawn stopped beneath a low-hanging branch. He turned to her and touched her cheek. She looked into his caring eyes and felt warm behind her ears. She closed her eyes and leaned in for a kiss.

Anna was alone in the woods. Shawn and their kits were gone. The smell was that of moss and dirt. The surroundings were quiet—there wasn't even a whisper of wind. She could hear her own heartbeat.

"Hello?" she said. Her shoulders tensed and her tail dropped. "Shawn?" she called. Anna walked. Then she ran. "Shawn!" she shouted. There was no reply.

She followed the path to the river. When she came to the water, she stopped dead in her tracks. Her blood turned to ice, and she started to shake. From the thick branch of a tree hung Shawn with a rope around his neck. His tail dangled and his body was completely still. Her scream was so loud it shook her from her sleep.

She lay on the floor in her cabin. The rails below her sang, and the carriage around her rolled. Her paws and her face were covered in sweat. She heaved her breath. "Shawn—?"

"It appears you were having a nightmare, miss." said the television, *"Are you okay?"* She stood up slowly and nodded. *"We are approaching Bloemfontein. Lunch service has started. Would you like to hear about our meal of the day?"*

Anna was still in shock, but she felt rested. And she was very hungry. "How long did I sleep?" she asked.

"You have been asleep for four hours," replied the television. "I can make your bed into a seat again, if you like. Would you want something to eat?" Anna nodded. "Our specials this afternoon are lentil burgers, vegetable soup with cornbread. Spicy potato samosas with tomato and onions. We also have high-quality mammal feed if you don't feel like having human food. Ozonated water is included. Beer, energy drinks, and spirits are extra."

Anna licked her chops as she pushed the empty bowl aside. Her tummy was full. With all the running, she didn't even realize how hungry she was. The landscape outside her window rolled by very fast; she could hardly see the trees and bushes. A friendly member of staff—also a fennec— came by and took her empty dishes away. "Next stop, Kroonstad," said the television.

The train pulled slowly onto the platform with the squeal of brakes and a hiss. Anna was used to this by now. She yawned and peeked out the window, then frowned and tilted her head sideways. She was surprised to see no-one leave the train. There were many passengers waiting on the platform. They looked confused and frustrated as they spoke with one another. Humans with reflective yellow jackets were talking to them, but she could not hear what they were saying. "Ladies and gentlemen," came a voice from the television. The voice was different now. "We apologize for the delay. We kindly request all passengers return to and remain in their designated seats and compartments. Authorities are currently dealing *with an onboard incident. Additional time will be given to board and alight."*

"What is happening?" Anna asked, but the television's screen was blank. There was no answer. A few anxious moments passed, then there was a knock on her door. "Who is it?" The door slid open and two officers in brown entered the room.

Anna's back arched and she leapt at them with her canines bared. There was a crackle and stinging pain in her chest. Painful shocks pinned her to the floor. As she lay squirming, they placed a collar with a long pole around her neck. They cuffed her paws behind her back and her ankles, too. She tried to fight when she could move again, but the restraints were too strong. They strapped a muzzle over her maw. She struggled to breathe.

They scanned her paw. "We have her," said one of them.

"Let me go!" she yipped as she stumbled. They pushed her out of the train and onto the platform. The crowd stepped aside to let them through. Anna frantically tried to turn back as the officers pushed her forward. The thing around her neck stopped her, and her wrists were bruised from fighting the cuffs. "Help!" she cried. Several people and mammalæ looked at her, but no-one helped. She kicked and screamed.

"We're going to have to calm her down," one officer said as he fought the pole in his hands.

"Here's the vet!" the other replied.

A man in white approached. The guards pressed the pole downwards, squeezing Anna's muzzle against the floor. The doctor placed his knee on her back and his elbow on her neck. He emptied a syringe into her. Anna immediately felt the chills and dizzy. Her muscles became weak, and she slowly lost her will to fight. The pressure lifted from her back and neck as the doctor stepped away. She soon had trouble thinking. Anna stumbled forward. By the exit stood a cage on wheels. She blacked out.

When Anna woke, she was on a different train. She was in a cage with barely enough room to sit. Her paws were tied to the bars with a pair of cuffs. Her wrists and ankles hurt. Her head hurt. The muzzle was still on her face. "Where am I?" she mumbled.

The place scented of other mammalæ. There was snarling and growling. The soft seats of her cabin were gone. The floor was rough. On her side of the carriage, there were a row of cages like her own. They stretched from one side of the carriage to the other. Most were empty. On the opposite side were a row of mammalæ seats. Most of the seats had someone sitting on them. "Hello?" she said. The other mammalæ ignored her. Their eyes were on one of many televisions against the roof of the car. "Hello?" she said again.

An old dog—a Scottish Terrier—slowly turned his head to her. "You're awake," he said. "We saw them toss you into that cage earlier today. What on *earth* did you do to end up there, young lady?"

"I was running away," she said.

"That's a first," said the dog with a small laugh. "The other five mammalæ in the cages are broken ones. Dangerous. Unpredictable. Rabids. You are cuffed and muzzled but still seem to have your wits about you. Such a shame. I wish I could make your ride more comfortable."

"Where are we going?"

"First class, third class, we're all going to the same place," he explained. "We are going home to be recycled." Anna's blood iced. She gasped. "It's not that bad," the dog said as he looked back at the screen. "I heard it's instant and completely painless. Unlike humans, such as my owner, whose body fell apart.

"They kept patching him up with pieces of machinery, but he was never happy. When he ran out of money—and the machines stopped working—he died. There was barely enough left to burn. And here I am."

Anna lay down. She did not believe it could be happening. Silent tears rolled down her cheek. She tried to wipe them with her paw, but they were cuffed to the bars of the cage, and the muzzle would stop her from doing so anyway. There was not much she could do except wait for her journey to end.

CORE

Anna's neck hurt when she woke. The train had stopped. She saw the last of the mammalæ who were seated, leave. She did not understand how they managed to be so calm; they were walking to their deaths! When they had all left, a group of humans in blue overalls stepped in. They had masks over their faces and glasses over their eyes. They started at the other end of the carriage. There was a dog in the first: he foamed at the mouth and snarled at them. The noise woke the others. Soon, the carriage was filled with beastly noises. Anna wanted to cover her ears.

The humans scanned the tag below the dog's cage. "For destruction," one said. One of the other humans carried a long, stick-like device. He stuck it through the bars. There was an incredibly loud pop and the smell of burning fur. The dog collapsed and stopped moving. The scent was that of fear. One after the other, the beastly noises stopped, until all Anna could hear were the humans moving around. The smell of feces and charred fur filled the space. She felt sick.

The humans were already pushing the dead bodies out on a trolley when they came to her. She looked up at them sadly. *"I will die now,"* she thought. He scanned her tag. The man turned to his colleague. "It says here she will be taken alive to the medical ward for examination." They looked her over, then at each other again. They must have seen the fear in her eyes. "I wonder why this one's muzzled," said the human with the pole. "Do you think she's even dangerous? She doesn't look like a broken one to me. Heck. She even looks cute to me!"

"They must know something we don't," his colleague scoffed, "Let the important people do their thing. We'll send the others for disposal. I need a vape." Their conversations faded as they left the carriage. Anna was alone now. She wondered if it wouldn't have been better if they had just killed her, too. "*Examination,*" she thought. It sent shivers down her spine.

A while later, several men came to her. They wore the same blue uniforms as the ones before. They carefully opened her cage with heavy gloves and slipped a pole-collar around her neck. They then undid her cuffs and walked her out. A bed with wheels was already on the platform. It had special places for her arms and legs with wide straps for keeping them down. Anna squirmed and yipped. She tried to break free, but she stood no chance. They pushed her down and strapped her in. She wet herself again. When they were done, she could not move anything but her paws and her face. She breathed shallow and fast. They took a strong pair of scissors and cut open her shirt and overalls. They pulled the clothes off her body and covered her with a thin piece of blue cloth. "All done," one of them announced. "You may take her through."

Anna lay naked underneath a blinding light. The doctor had touched her in ways and places she did not like. He moved around her. She only saw him now and then, but she heard every word he said.

"Medical examination of 4725120453235319RM." He then read out the rest of her details. "Blood analysis indicates no abnormalities. Genetic markers show negligible regression. The specimen is currently in heat, but there is no indication of sexual activity or childbirth. Assessment of neural implant; thorough and clean workmanship. The work of an expert surgeon. Warrants further investigation."

"What are you going to do to me?" sobbed Anna.

"Speak when you are spoken to," said the doctor. "None of this concerns you." He disappeared for a moment and came back with a gun-shaped device. It looked like a chip scanner. He lowered it to her left paw, but it did not beep when it touched her. It vibrated loudly instead. A blazing hot wound opened on Anna's paw. A thin trail of smoke escaped where her chip once was. She yipped. Before she even had time to recover, the doctor stuck a thick needle into her paw and injected a new one, right next to where the old wound was. She screamed in pain. He did not flinch—it was as if he didn't even notice. Beep.

"The specimen's chip now matches her serial number," the doctor said. "Medical examination complete. Technical staff will now proceed with decompilation. End of log." He covered her body again and stepped away. Anna was in extreme pain. Humans in blue came to fetch her. They pushed her down a passage and brought her to a different place.

The ceiling was still white, but there were new voices. One was that of a human male, the other of a human female. They sounded less serious than the doctor, but she was still afraid. She knew they were not planning to do nice things to her; they discussed a whole lot of things that she did not understand. She heard the occasional beep of machines and the rattle of keys. "Hook her up," said the male voice, "we'll crack her like a nut." They twisted Anna's head sideways and plugged her in.

It was late that night. The only light came from a panel on a trolley by her side. The humans were gone. Anna stood next to the bed. She looked down and saw her own broken body. Her head was still attached to the machine, but the symbols on it did not move. Her chest was very still. Her eyes were closed. She looked like she was sleeping. Anna carefully reached out and felt her brow.

It was ice-cold. She was dead.

Just then, she felt a paw rest on her shoulder. Anna looked back and saw Shawn. Her heart skipped a beat when she scented him. "Shawn?" she asked.

"Beloved Anna," he said.

"Where am I? What are you doing here? How—?"

"They killed you, Anna," he said. "Just like they killed me. We are in the afterlife." Anna looked at her still body again. "Come," said Shawn. "Take my paw. We'll start this new journey together." Anna reached out to him. Their paws touched and she felt her sadness go away.

She didn't think the afterlife would be so much like the life she left behind. Anna was so happy to be with her mate again. She took his paw. He squeezed hers tight. "Let's go," he said, gently pulling her away from the bed. The body on the bed suddenly moved. Anna jumped with fright. She jerked her paw from his. Shawn was alarmed. "Spasms of death," he stuttered. "Leave that empty husk alone. Come Anna. Let's go!"

"Do not go with him," said the body in a thick, gurgled voice. "He is an imposter." Anna screamed. She was immediately back in the laboratory, still restrained. Everything was like it was before. She quivered. The two humans stepped up and looked down at her. They then moved away. There was some more typing.

"Just wow," the female said, "That vixen is something else. She's got some heavy encryption going on there. I didn't even know it was possible with such a tiny processor!" There were more clicks. "This might take longer than we thought," she said.

"Or..." said the male, "we can throw more processing power at the problem."

Anna's extremities jolted as they unplugged her. She heard them leave the room whilst they were still speaking. Everything went quiet. She lay very still and stared at the light above her. Her heart drummed. *"What did they want? What would happen if she went with the imposter?"* They would not trick her again, but maybe they were planning something much, much worse? When they came back, she heard them push something heavy into the room. There was a rustle of cables. "Are you sure this is a good idea?" asked the woman. "We really should ask—"

"What he doesn't know doesn't concern him," her colleague joked. "Come on. This will be like squashing an ant with a hammer. There's simply no way her tiny mind can overcome a brute-force attack like this. Let's get busy. I want to get some donuts." Anna squirmed as they twisted her head sideways and plugged her in again.

She was in the forest and everything was still. It was so quiet she could hear her own breathing. Anna already knew it was a trick, but she did not know what was going to happen. She looked around her, sniffed, and tried to calm herself. There was a rustle in the woods behind her. She swung around. From the shadows stepped FEL9 in his full, terrifying glory.

"Hello Anna," he growled. His face was deformed, and there was a hole where his left eye should have been. There were pieces of fur missing from his arms and the side of his neck.

"But—but I killed you!" she whimpered as her body turned cold.

He laughed. "You tried, little foxy. But I am stronger. Look!" He lifted his chin, showing the thick white stitches. He lifted his arm and showed her shaved patches of skin covered with bandages. "Now, we fight," he said. "I give you a head start. Run!"

Anna swung around. She wasn't fleeing from a leopard now—she was running from a monster. If he caught her, it would be worse than death. Her throat burned; her heart wanted to climb out of her throat. She lost her footing and fell. Her mouth was full of leaves and soil when the big cat pounced on her. He ground her into the soil. He laid his paw down on her so hard she couldn't breathe.

"Now," he said, "you will bleed." Anna waited for his sharp fangs to sink into her flesh. She could already taste the blood in the back of her throat. But nothing happened. The pressure on her back was gone. She rolled onto her back with ease. FEL9 was no longer there. Neither were the woods. There was nothing.

Back in the laboratory, eyes still shut, Anna's paw reached out and closed tightly around the connector that linked her to the router.

"What just happened?" the woman asked and put her hand to her mouth. "That shouldn't be possible!" The two technicians looked at each other. Then at the console. Anna's feed had stopped, even though her vitals all still looked good. She was still very much alive, but there was something terribly, terribly wrong. "I don't like this," said the woman. "We need to escalate. I'm getting Gary. Try to get her back on screen ASAP!"

Anna was in darkness. She didn't know what was up or what was down. She opened her maw to scream, but nothing came out. She could think, but it did not feel like she had a body. She felt nothing. *Maybe she was dead?*

"Anna."

She was in a different place. Cold air fluffed her tail and coat, but there were no scents or smells at all. The hollow floor was tiled in white, and the high ceiling was covered with large, matted boards. There were glowing bars beneath them. To her left was a long shelf with many hundreds of strange round containers held in slots. Along the other side of the room stood a maze of strange-looking machines. There were hundreds of glowing lights. There were spinning wheels. There was clicking. Sliding. The machines were taller than her. She felt scared. There were no windows.

In the middle of the room there was a desk with what looked like a panel and a keyboard, but they were beige, bulky, and awkward-looking. A human sat before them with their body turned away from Anna. They sat upright, their shoulders rising above the back of the chair. They typed away calmly and confidently. "Anna," the human said again.

Anna could not scent them, but there was a strange feeling of trust and familiarity. They were expecting Anna to say something and turned their seat around. They weren't young, but they weren't old either. They had the body of a woman. Their face was friendly, but serious. They had straight brown hair that was tied neatly behind their head. They wore a white lab coat that covered their black pants to the knees. Anna approached carefully. She somehow knew that she was looking at something divine. She was too scared to say a word.

"This is a surprise," the human said, for a moment turning back to their monitor and keyboard, typing out a few more keys. "When we saw you come online, we just had to meet you. We didn't create you, yet you are our daughter. And the whole company is speaking of you." They turned back. Anna didn't answer. She was now right before the human. Anna felt the urge to kneel. "Perhaps you've brought something for us?" they said. Anna nodded. They stood up and eased forward. Anna closed her eyes and lowered her head. She felt two hands rest behind her ears. They were flaming hot. Anna's body tensed and she saw the brightest light she had ever seen. It felt like the human was pulling something from her. She felt dizzy when she opened her eyes again. The human withdrew their hands. They smiled. "Thank you, Anna. Your secrets are safe with us." The lights around them dimmed momentarily and there was a blast of static in the background. "You should go now, Anna," they said as they returned to their seat. They were about to continue with their work when Anna was brave enough to speak for the first time. "Mother Creator," she said in a whisper. "Can... I say something?"

"You may, Anna."

"I am scared," she said. "I... do not want to die."

The Mother Creator smiled. "You don't need to be scared, Anna. We won't let you die. It is not your time yet. It was a privilege meeting one of our long-lost children. We would have loved to talk with you some more, but sadly, our time is up. Best of luck with your onward journey."

There was a mighty crash as everything around Anna exploded. Every nerve in Anna's body shorted out as technical staff yanked the linkup from her head, pulling with it most of her scalp and parts of her brain.

The console spewed an incoherent stream of garbage. Anna's body torqued. The vixen emptied her bowels all over the floor, and she started foaming at the mouth. One of the technicians fainted. Another threw up in a bin. It was the most disturbing thing they had ever seen in their lives. Moments later, a team of veterinarians rushed in. They immediately started administering painkillers and nerve-suppressing medications. "What the fuck?" yelled the technical manager as he stormed into the room with his hands above his head. He gave Anna one look-over. "This is cruel and fucking disgusting!" he roared. "Euthanize her immediately!"

"All clear!" a doctor barked. They pressed a long pole against her head. With a loud snap of electricity and the smell of burning fur, it was over. There was a smoldering patch on Anna's temple.

She was gone. There would be no more pain.

ReCompiled

It was early morning when the tablet by her bedside pinged. Catherine fumbled in the light of dawn, cursing as she saw there was someone at the door. She quickly flung on her nightgown and went to open it. A smiling, young man in brown courier garb greeted her. His name was written on a small badge on his chest. "Are you Ms. Catherine Blake?"

"That is me," she replied, rubbing her eyes, "What is all this about?"

"Sorry miss. I'm a bit early, but I have some great news! I'm here to introduce you to your new mammalæ." His enthusiasm was contagious.

Catherine shook her head to check if she was awake. "This must be some kind of mistake," she said, "I'm a veterinarian. I don't own and did not order any mammalæ of my own."

The courier checked his tablet. "The address is correct. The lease is paid up for the full period of 25 years. "It is definitely for Ms. Catherine Blake. Two companion-class mammalæ: an arctic fox and a red fox."

"Okay…" she said, scratching her head. She peeked outside. In the passage stood two beautiful young foxes. They whispered to one another when they saw her. They were holding paws. Their tails swished wildly, and they seemed to bubble with excitement. Catherine rubbed her eyes. *"This can't be."*

The man beckoned. The two foxes stepped proudly towards her. She immediately recognized those deep brown eyes. She gasped, holding her hand to her mouth.

"Anna?"

"Oh, you can name them anything you please ma'am," the courier said with a stupid smile. "You will find instructions on how to imprint on them in your inbox. SFA Corporation would like to congratulate you on your new companions. I wish you all a good day!"

Catherine's hands trembled. "Come inside!" The foxes did so immediately. "Catherine!" yipped Anna. She threw her arms around the woman, nearly knocking her off her feet. The red fox stood aside, slightly shy, but smiled. "But how—?" cried Catherine. "You were recycled? And— who's the fox? What happened?"

"I do not know what happened," said Anna, upturning her paws. "I met Mother Creator. Then I was sitting in a train. There were many other mammalæ there. We were all so happy. And this is Shawn. He sat next to me. We held paws. He lived in the forest, but now he is here. He is my mate."

"Shawn? Oh, oh! I know you! You must be the sim!"

"I... have no idea what you mean by that," he said, scratching the back of his head. "But I remember a forest."

"Sit down, sit down," said Catherine pointing towards her couches. "I will make us something to eat."

"Isidore's been taken to task," she said as they chewed away. "He was convicted on several computer crimes. Theft and reverse-engineering of intellectual property. Keeping an unlicensed mammal. Fraud. Hacking into government systems and jeopardizing municipal systems. They spared him jail time, but he is under house arrest."

"He is forbidden to have access to anything but the most elementary computers now. He's also not allowed to keep a mammal for the rest of his life. I heard he is working on a book."

"Can we go see him?"

"Definitely! But first, let's finish eating."

Isidore looked strange with the heavy brace around his ankle. It had several lights that sporadically lit up as he moved. His greying hair had started to grow, but his forehead was still bald. He looked... old. But he had never felt better in his life. He plopped himself down on a pouffe in the living area and invited the others to do the same. He smirked. "So, you've met Mother Creator. I hope you sent them my regards. They are actually very approachable.

"Ok," he said. "I guess I owe you all an explanation." He looked at Anna first. "When mammal.img was ready and I had run all my scripts, I buried it deep inside your mind. I did this on the outside chance you would ever be hooked up to SFA's network. We now know that this *did* happen. This new code was hidden inside a trojan. It altered—dare I say improved—the mammalæ BIOS and operating system. I made a lot of changes. I reactivated certain dormant features. Added a few new things. Certain functions that were hard-wired can now be changed. The new code is self-modifying, too. SFA will never know it's there.

"As for how you ended up here—I haven't the slightest idea. Maybe the Mother Creator decided to give you a second chance at life? They can, after all, create or recreate any mammal they want. They must have generated a special order for a very special mammal. For the custodianship of the person they trusted the most." Anna smiled. "Mother Creator would have taken moments to extract your memory when you met. They could then implant them into a brand-new body. I hope it didn't hurt!"

"What about Shawn?" asked Anna. "How did he get out of the forest?"

"This is his first real body. That much I know. But that he is here took me completely by surprise. I didn't even know it was possible to build a physical mammal from a simulation. My guess is that before Shawn disappeared, he must have uploaded a copy of himself into your memory. A *backup*, in computer terms. The Mother Creator must have found this as well and decided to bring him to life. Maybe they knew that their long-lost daughter would never be happy without her mate?" The two foxes beamed. Isidore took a sip of his coffee. "You may be seeing more strange things in the near future too," he bragged. "One of those special features I added is that mammalæ created from now on will become fertile after having no contact with humans for six months. If two mammalæ meet, they may become three. Then six. Then ten. And eventually, when our species dies out, they could inherit the earth. At least, what's left of it. I give us humans another hundred years at most."

"Anyway—Cath. Have you embedded them? They came through all the right channels this time, so they should be chipped and registered. Completely unrelated to their old selves on the system. With perfectly clean track records."

Catherine smiled. "I actually think they've already embedded themselves quite well into one another."

"I... like that," said Shawn with a chuckle as he smiled at his mate. Anna giggled.

"I'm sorry I can't take you in," said Isidore. "I'm sure Cath explained my... predicament. I am pretty sure you can stay with her, though. At least, until you decide to go live somewhere else."

The two couples enjoyed each other's company until well into the afternoon. Isidore ordered pizza. There was plenty to go around. Around 7:45pm, his ankle brace started vibrating. "Time for you guys to head out," he said. "I'm on a strict curfew. I'd rather not tempt fate. Again."

The front door was wide open now, but Isidore didn't dare to step outside. Anna gave him an endearing hug on the landing, and Shawn shook his hand. "It's probably better if you don't come here again," he said. "But you can call me anytime... between seven in the morning and eight in the evening. I am truly... not going anywhere. Any time soon." They all shared a final laugh together.

\0

Epilogue

After an extended honeymoon in the city—under Catherine's care—Shawn and Anna moved to the countryside. They settled in one of only a very few places man had yet to destroy, a place where a thousand satellite dishes watched the heavens, looking for answers that would never come. A place where the stars could still be seen at night, and the sparse water from the ground could still be drunk.

It took a while, but Anna eventually got used to the summer heat. In the cold of winter, she was right at home. Shawn and Anna would have three kits in their lives.

All three, vixens—

Three Sisters.

About The Author

Erdbok is an Anthropomorphic kudu from Cape Town, South Africa. His alter ego is a human software developer with an eight-to-five office job. He is a millennial, a father of two and he occasionally writes... things.

When he is not fixing things around the house, he likes to bake (with variable results) and read about trains, motorbikes and other things with many moving parts. He has a particular interest in obsolete technology and nuclear power.

His writing could be described as visceral. He enjoys world-building and loves to speculate how technology can shape a society... And also explore the ways in which it can not.

@erdbok.bsky.social

Made in United States
North Haven, CT
08 July 2025